# *The Trail Back Out*

## BY THE SAME AUTHOR

*Broken In: A Novel in Stories*
*Tsunami Cowboys*
*Grounded*

### FOR THE STAGE

*I Like a Gershwin Tune, How About You?*
*Hard Times in Sugar Town*
*One Page Plays: Bank On It; Baby You Were Great*

# *The Trail Back Out*

Short Stories

by

Jadi Campbell

Text Copyright © 2020 Jadi Campbell
Cover Art Copyright © 2014 Walter Share
All rights reserved
ISBN: 9798671840049
First Edition: August 2020
Contact: jadi.campbell@t-online.de
jadicampbell.com

For my sisters,
Pamela Jean and Barbara Lee

## Contents

Quack Quack ..................................................................11

Better Weather ...............................................................45

Rules To Live By ............................................................51

The River ........................................................................61

What Died in the Fridge ...............................................69

The Red Wallet ..............................................................79

Princess Rain Clouds ....................................................85

Do Dreams Float? ........................................................117

The Green Under the Snow ........................................127

The Trail Back Out ......................................................133

Afterword .....................................................................163

On they went through thick forests where the sun never shone, over rivers so wide that it took a whole day to sail across them, up hills whose sides were all of glass; on they went through seven times seven countries till Peter reined in his horse before the house of an old woman.

'Good day, mother,' he said, jumping down and opening the door.

'Good day, my son,' answered she, 'and what are you doing here, at the world's end?'

– *Eisenkopf, The Crimson Fairy Book*

# QUACK QUACK

For the first time in his life, Lorrie used a barf bag. He threw up as they circled in the airspace over Venice. He was terribly seasick. Airsick? Plane sick? His mind wandered. He needed a second barf bag before they landed. Once the plane touched the tarmac, he rushed to the bathroom cabin to brush his teeth and rinse out his mouth with bottled water.

"Welcome to Marco Polo Airport. We are sincerely glad to be back on the ground; it was one bumpy flight. Thank you for flying Air Italia." A bumpy flight indeed. Make that, flights. While the captain spoke, the flight crew smiled tired, tired smiles. "We hope to fly with you again soon," the captain told him. Lorrie almost hit his head as he went out the narrow door.

A voice calling his name broke through his brain fog when he entered the terminal. "Laurence? Lorrie? Laurence James! Over here."

He stumbled and fell over an old Italian couple wheeling matching luggage behind them.

"Look at you!" Suzanna exclaimed as she helped him back up.

He obliged her and looked down. Little carrot bits from a flight meal clung to the bottom of his shirt; hastily he wiped them away. He stood back and admired her.

Her charcoal gray pantsuit was of quality cloth and she wore low-heeled sandals. She had thrown a scarf over her blond hair.

She was radiant.

If he hadn't known better, Lorrie would have mistaken her for a local; she didn't look a bit like an American. They kissed and he breathed in her now familiar, slightly spicy perfume. Lorrie felt more awake: the trip could finally begin. Then he realized she was by herself. "You didn't bring Juliet?"

"No, darling. She knows I'm bringing a friend for her to meet when she gets home from school. It's her last term before we go back to America for good, and it took her forever to get ready for *that* change." She ran a hand over his gray hair, clipped short but still full. "You're so distinguished-looking! She'll love you." She cupped his narrow face for a few loving seconds. "I booked us a water taxi. It's romantic to see Venice for the first time from a boat, even in bad weather. Actually, especially in bad weather."

"I might be too jetlagged to appreciate the details." They exited the small airport building. Lorrie dragged his suitcase through the rain and tried to keep up with the sweetheart he had flown halfway around the world to see.

Suzanna had a bad, failed marriage behind her. After a whirlwind courtship, the shock of Giovanni's expectations of her as a brood mare (as she put it) and the nightmare of her horrible cooking (as he put it), plus their almost total incompatibility in politics, religion, and 'what defines reality' (as both put it), they finally divorced, years after the birth of their single child.

Juliet was born in a hospital in Verona, and what other name could there be for a girl child birthed in that noble city? Giovanni's parents lived on the mainland outside Venice. Naturally, Suzanna brought their grandchild to visit. It was inevitable, perhaps, that she fell in love with the improbability of Venice. She loved its streets of water, the way the light flickered over the canals. She adored the city's absurd beginnings in a swamp and centuries as the greatest mercantile power on the planet.

Suzanna and Lorrie came from the same small Vermont city and had reconnected via social media. An only child,

Suzanna went to be by her father's side when he fell ill. She hated not getting to take Juliet, but her daughter was on the school soccer team. Juliet had assured her that she'd be fine, just fine. Suzanna emailed Lorrie to say she would be in town.

Lorrie came to the hospital. She spent all her free time with him on the first trip and every visit after that. When her father died, she inherited everything; she flew back several times to sort out the estate. Lorrie proposed, and she said yes.

And now here he was, in Venice. "Here's the water taxi pier. Watch your step. And don't worry about acqua alta. Our apartment is on the third floor, so we stay dry."

"What's that?" Lorrie slid on the slippery boat deck and almost fell as he climbed into the water taxi. They rode in the choppy waves away from the pier, and his stomach felt queasy. He had moved through unstable elements for the better part of thirty hours.

The boat stopped at the Rialto Mercado pier an eternity later. Suzanna thanked the boatman in liquid-sounding Italian. *How does she do that?* Lorrie wondered. When they first planned to rendezvous in Venice, he purchased a guidebook with language phrases; enrolled in a beginners' Italian class at the local community college; conceded defeat and quit after the fourth class. What kind of language made you stretch your face this way? He had smiled with all the sincerity a man could muster until his jaw ached. He attempted the bewildering ch-, zz-, and vowel combinations aio-!, glio!- and realized he would *never* learn any Italian.

Lorrie stumbled off the water taxi, ridiculously happy to feel hard cobblestones under his feet.

Suzanna led him into an alley. At an entryway identical to all the others on the street, she opened a wooden door. They mounted a narrow marble staircase. "Too bad your flight was so late. I bought us croissants and fruit for a *real* breakfast! You'll be horrified at what Italians eat for breakfast. Rolls made of air and a little sugar. They're just foils for an espresso," she informed him over her shoulder.

He wrestled his bag around a bend in the hallway.

"Here we are." She unlocked an apartment door. "Juliet?" The apartment, overly warm, consisted of three rooms with marble floors. Suzanna opened a door and poked her head in a small room with a single bed. "Juliet's bedroom." She led him on to the sitting room. The furniture consisted of two ancient worm-holed walnut chests against the back wall, a new television, and a deep couch and three matching chairs upholstered in faded green velvet. Rain lashed the closed tall windows.

Suzanna picked up a torn page of notepaper lying on the chest by the sofa. "Mom, I'm at Isabella's. We have practice later. Hugs and kisses, Jules," she read aloud. "She's got soccer, so I guess we're on our own this afternoon." She didn't sound terribly disappointed. "It's not like she's trying to avoid meeting you. Juliet doesn't 'know' about you yet anyway. We have Wi-Fi," she added, apropos of nothing.

She took his damp suitcase from him and dragged it into the master bedroom where she set it by one of the two single beds. Suzanna could sense Lorrie's disappointment. "We can push the beds together later," she consoled him.

The bathroom was surprisingly modern with white tiles and a functioning shower. Next, she showed him the tiny kitchen. "Just a refrigerator and hot burner? Where's the stove?"

"We like to eat out. I was married to an Italian, but don't want to slave in a kitchen myself! But the Rialto Mercado is close if you want fresh produce or seafood."

He kissed the side of her ear. "Right. Once I get some sleep I'll think straight again."

"You're probably dehydrated. Drink this," she ordered, and waited as he emptied a large glass of fresh orange juice that was a strange, deep red. "Let me run out and get some things, how about cheese and mortadella and bread, we already have croissants and fruit, we'll just do a picnic lunch. A getting-to-know-you meal with Juliet can wait." She kissed him deeply and Lorrie felt the stirrings of desire.

Hopeful, he placed a hand on her breast. "Wait on the picnic?"

She pushed his hand away. "I need to get groceries before shops close for a few hours. Rest a little bit," she suggested. "I'll be right back, don't go anywhere!"

"Not a chance." Suzanna pulled the heavy velvet curtains halfway and the room darkened. He stretched out on the couch and closed his eyes. The cushions scratched. Horsehair? She draped his body with a blanket. Lips brushed his left shoulder and the door closed quietly as she let herself out.

Like sex, sleep was only a wistful desire. In his head Lorrie still sat on planes, flying towards a difficult future event. He sat back up and a wave of motion vertigo washed over him. He was going to be violently sick all over the sofa.

He made it to the bathroom and bid farewell to the glass of blood orange juice. His haggard face looked back in the bathroom's fluorescent lights. Lorrie put his head under the faucet and ran stale water over his face. He was sweating. Back in the living room he removed his food-speckled pants and wrinkled shirt and stretched back out on the cushions. The sofa sagged. The room kept spinning until he closed his eyes.

He turned on his side and began to snore the sleep of the exhausted, the innocent and the helpless. He woke at the rasp of a key in the lock and sound of the door opening. Lorrie held out his arms, eyes still closed. "Come to Papa," he growled.

The lights switched on and someone screamed. He opened his eyes and an adolescent girl stood in front of the door. Blond hair waved down over her shoulders and the wet team jacket she wore. She carried a sagging bag filled with cans.

Lorrie sat up. "Did I drop off? What time is it?" He stood up, blinking as he tried to shake off his stupor. The girl stared, and hastily he draped the fringed blanket around himself like a toga. He held out a hand. "You must be Julia."

Her blue eyes widened. "Don't come near me! The police are on the way! We have no jewels!" It sounded like *jools*; it sounded like her name. She began to hurl sodas.

"*Hey*! What the heck?" Lorrie's arms flailed and the blanket dropped to the floor. He tried to parry the metal hitting his body. "Stop! I'm not a burglar!"

The last can fell to the floor and when Juliet kicked it, the can flew through the room and bounced hard off the side of Lorrie's head.

A key turned in the door for the second time in three minutes.

"You're in a robber *band*!" she shrieked. Out of ammunition, Juliet whirled. She fought the doorknob as it turned under her hand. Suzanna finally managed to push in through the door that Juliet, still shrieking, was trying to hold closed.

"Juliet! It's okay!" Suzanna couldn't hold both the wrapped packages and the doorknob, so she dropped her picnic items.

"There's a burglar in here!"

Suzanna held her trembling daughter. "Everything's all right!"

"Everything's not all right!"

"Calm down! What happened to soccer practice?"

"It got cancelled, it rained all day, in case you haven't noticed!"

"Juliet! Don't sass your mother."

"And I came home and found a pervert!"

"He's not a pervert, I know him!"

"Mom, his *clothes* are off! He stood up and I saw basically everything!"

"I just told you: I know him. Wait! What did you say?" Her head swiveled. "You took your clothes off?"

"I thought it was you coming back in!"

"You *know* him?"

"Lorrie, why are you in your underwear?"

"The room was too hot. I thought it would be easier to sleep if I got undressed. I dozed off."

"Did you take off your clothes before or after you thought it was me?"

"Before. I kept my underwear on!" He hunched over, wrapping the blanket back around his body.

"Are you bleeding?" Suzanna looked more closely at her lover. She turned back to her daughter. "Juliet, this is the visitor I was telling you about."

"You told me you were bringing your friend Laura home!"

"Laurence. Friends call me Lorrie. And you must be Juliet." He put out his hand and the blanket dropped again.

"You're no lady." She put her hands behind her back and stepped further away. "You're a guy. Mom, he put out his arms and said, 'Come to Papa!'"

Suddenly her mother was laughing so hard she almost fell. "Come to Papa?" Suzanna groped her way to a chair.

In the middle of the room a punctured soda can slowly rolled and fizzed out the last of its contents onto the floor tiles. Lorrie perched on the sofa with the fringed blanket wrapped back around his waist like a travesty of a flamenco dancer.

"Let's start over." Grinning, Suzanna handed Lorrie his clothes from where they lay in a heap beside the sofa. "Juliet. I'd like you to meet Laurence James Heples, he goes by Lorrie. I am so sorry; I had no idea you thought the special friend I wanted you to meet was a girl. A lady. I'm *sure* the first time I mentioned Lorrie I told you his name's Laurence James."

"You always came back from Vermont laughing! You told me, you'd hooked back up with someone who was like your best friend and favorite person in the whole world (except for me), all rolled into one. You said Laurie was coming to spend a month with us before we move to Vermont. And the three of us would enjoy being together in Venice because this is a fun place. You said, we'd see a lot of each other once we go to Vermont." Juliet slowly came away from the door. She remained on tiptoes, hovering. Maybe she would race out. Maybe she was about to kick the winning goal of a ball game being played for stakes not yet defined or decided.

"Well," announced Lorrie, "this took care of the jet lag… that might be the last time I ever fall asleep!"

☐

Juliet retrieved the sodas while her mother bandaged Lorrie's bleeding head. "Wow! My aim sure is good! Those places where those cans hit your legs are going to leave some *big* old bruises," she proudly declared. "But, the rain's stopped, so let's go show you Venice!"

"How about a picnic? You can decide where we take Lorrie to dinner later, Juliet," Suzanna suggested.

Out on the street, Juliet took charge. "So, *you're* my mom's friend! From the way she talked about Laurie, I was *sure* you had to be an old *lady* who breathes through her nose funny! Mom always talked about a great friend and all the *fun* you have together. Though I wondered a lot, what were two old ladies doing playing together?"

"Juliet, it's rude to call somebody old when they're not. Say, grown up. Or, mature."

Juliet rolled her eyes. "How about *middle* aged? Though it

is really *amazing* to me, now that I'm almost thirteen, it feels like old isn't quite what it *used* to be. When I was a *little* kid, say, half as old as I am now, I just *knew* once I became a double-digiter it was going to make me feel old. It didn't, it just means that I have to act mature or something. Like you say Mom, I'm not a *baby* anymore. You and Lorrie *can't* be old yet even though from here it sure *seems* that way, in another, forty years or something, I don't know, the two of you will just seem, *normal* old or something."

Juliet decided that Lorrie wasn't a burglar, but he might still be dangerous, a threat to her standing in the family as undisputed center point. She was determined to dominate him through the combined force of her personality and an unending barrage of conversation. "So where to go tonight … do you guys feel like *pizza*, or do you feel like *pasta*? The Trattoria Pescia has *delicious* fried calamaries. And around the corner from them is the Ristorante La Laguna, but Mom says they charge you just for looking at the menus. They have a cat that lives in the back of the restaurant and always comes over to my chair. He likes to take food from my hand and never ever bites my fingers. Oh! Lorrie, two blocks that way is my favorite chocolates shop. They roll everything by hand. The mamma uses a recipe handed down in her family for like, three generations already! They use an almond paste and that is really delicious." Her arms waved as words poured from her mouth.

Lorrie tried to make sense of the situation. He wandered lost through her endless sentences; he couldn't orient himself in the twisting streets. He trailed behind as they crossed a bridge; most streets seemed to end at a ledge with canal water. All the little streets were crooked. Every few blocks the street names on house walls changed.

Alleys opened out to Venice's little piazzas with their fountains. Each crowded square was filled with tables and chairs for cafés and restaurants and ice cream shops.

Buildings with tall Moorish windows seemed to nod overhead, leaning towards one another to whisper, or to eavesdrop on Juliet's running lecture.

"You know what's really old? *Venice*. It's sinking! Venice is like, the prettiest city I've ever been in. Mom has really shown me the world, oh I *know* Italy isn't the *whole* world, but it sure is more than most of what all my friends back in the United States have seen. Although Cecilia and her family went camping all across the southwest and stayed in a bunch of really cool parks last summer. They rented a camper and everything! You can't camp here – shoot, people can't even *drive* in Venice. They don't have any *cars*, just boats. Although my mom says that's a good thing, because Italians drive like crazy people! It makes my dad really mad; Mom always tells him to slow the aitch ee double hockey sticks down if we're going somewhere together in a car when we visit him at my grandmother's. He just yells back at her in *Italian*. I always pretend like I don't know what he says. Italian has lots of really funny curse words."

"Jules," her mother warned mildly.

"Mom, my Italian teacher says my accent is excellent. I talk a lot but I never swear. Lorrie, if I get mad, I just go really, really silent." The girl crossed her arms over her chest and the flow of words ceased.

Suzanna touched the bandage, making sure it was still secure on Lorrie's forehead. "She's very sensitive to what other people think even though it seems like she never closes her mouth long enough to notice, much less take in any air. Don't let Juliet fool you. When she's offended, the stream of consciousness rap shuts like a tap. An exaggerated silence lets you know you've hurt her feelings. I don't know if she gets that from her father. People claim north Italians are more reserved, and Venetians can be snooty. But her grandfather's family comes from the Mezzogiorno, and my girl's a born actress."

"Mom, I already told you a million *times*. I can't be a movie star because I'm going to be a soccer star!" Juliet stamped her foot in frustration. "You need to *listen* more when I tell you things. I've decided we'll eat our picnic lunch across from that alley, in the pretty piazza over there."

Somehow he made it through the afternoon. On their way back to the pensione, Lorrie stumbled on the uneven cobble stones. He reached automatically for his lover's hand, but she was using it to carry the remains of their picnic. Juliet, in firm possession of the far hand, looked over at him in sly triumph. Far out on the horizon, towers of gray clouds stacked up on the Adriatic Sea.

He didn't sleep that night. Each time he turned in his little twin bed, Lorrie discovered another muscle that ached from Julia's can kicks. Cancan kicks, he thought tiredly.

The next day was warm and clear. When Juliet got home from school, Lorrie tried again. "How about I buy you something you've always wanted, so we can get back on the right foot with one another," he offered.

"Bribing your way into my child's affections?"

"Not really…." he answered slowly. "More like a peace offering to apologize for how bad I scared her yesterday. I *would* like to do something to let Juliet know how sorry I am."

Juliet bounced, excited. "I know! Buy me a mask. I was going to get one before we leave for America. Get me a traditional one. A *real* one."

Suzanna explained. "Most Venetian masks are mass-produced in China now. You don't need to do this, Lorrie. Genuine masks are expensive. Juliet, how about a bead necklace?"

"Mom, you promised I could get a real one at the end of the summer, why can't I get one now!"

"I'd *like* to buy it," Lorrie insisted, and smiled at Juliet.

She smiled back at him.

The three headed out for the center of the city. The

crowds swelled larger as they neared the Rialto Bridge. A swarm of Asian tourists slowed Lorrie's progress, all talking excitedly, their necks strung with cameras. Juliet planted herself in the middle of the alley. She waited like an impatient queen for an especially slow courtier who might become a royal favorite but would more likely end banished to the Bridge of Sighs.

A retiree stumped along right in front of Lorrie, using a cane topped with a carved duck head. The old man wore a fedora on his white hair and a knotted cravat in his vest. The Venetian kept on his way, using the cane for balance. He ignored the stream of tourists forced to slow behind him.

The hurrying world squeezed between the poles of the old man and Juliet. Babbling voices overwhelmed Lorrie's ears, already battered by waves of conversation gushing from a child with no filters. Bodies jostled. Impervious, Juliet went on talking as she waited for Lorrie to catch up.

He remained stuck just behind the well-dressed retiree.

An argument behind him got louder. "Dolan, go faster! We'll miss the tour!" a woman's voice insisted.

A pair of overweight middle-aged tourists in matching yellow ball caps and oversized white tee shirts with tour name tags reached him. The man who was Dolan pushed by and the bag hanging off his shoulder hit Lorrie square between the shoulder blades. Lorrie stumbled against the building; Dolan pressed on and shoved the retiree next.

The ancient Venetian lost his balance, but the press of the crowds kept him upright. He braced himself with a palm against a stone wall and raised the cane. He and Dolan glared at one another as the old man shook the cane. "E´ brutto!" he shouted. A curse in angry Venetian dialect followed.

"Quack quack quack!" Dolan mocked. He reached the corner as the streams of tourists surged forward and backward. The old man went on cursing. "Quack!" Dolan shouted a last time before he vanished.

Juliet had to wait in line to use the public toilet.

Those were their first quiet minutes since Lorrie's promised purchase. "She might be warming up to you," Suzanna said dryly. "Juliet and her friends only have cheap Chinese-made masks."

"It can't make all *that* much difference where they're produced, can it?"

Juliet heard his comment as she returned from the bathroom. "C'mere, silly." Juliet dragged him off by the hand to find a real mask.

She led him to a booth with a sign stating *Our masks are hand crafted*. A second sign on the side of the booth depicted a man with slanted eyes, a conical straw hat and a black line drawn through the middle of the cartoon. *No Chinese goods sold here!* the sign exclaimed in six languages.

Juliet tugged Lorrie's hand in excitement. She pointed at a row of dangling masks. "This one," she declared.

The vendor sitting at the back of the booth was working on an *Il Giorno* crossword puzzle. She was a middle-aged woman with short brown hair and large glasses. She wore small gold hoop earrings and despite how warm the afternoon was, she had wrapped her neck in a silk scarf. Down to the casual loafers on her feet, her outfit was immaculate.

She handed the mask to them to examine. The face was alabaster with swirls of purple, gold, and royal blue on the cheeks and along the edges. Blue lips matched the color around the eye slits.

Lorrie stroked the cloth cap sewn onto the brow. Stiff material curled forward into ends. The vendor bent them forward and back, showing him how the parts curled and he could adjust them for length and twist. It reminded him of a jester's cap. Gold braid outlined the ends and was stitched along the sides of the mask. The braid ended in a large jewel, high in the middle of the brow. A large pearl and a bell hung at each of the cap's five points. Actually, it looked *nothing* like a jester's cap.

The vendor turned it over and pointed out a stamp on the inside proving the mask had been made in Venice. Then she tied it firmly to the back of Juliet's head.

"It looks perfect," Suzanna commented in Italian and English. "What do you think?"

"Nice, but I still don't get it. What's the big deal?" Lorrie asked.

The adult women smiled at one another. "Just a couple thousand years of history. Each mask is special." Suzanna led him to the next aisle of hanging faces. "This one? See the funny chin? It's the volto, or larva."

"Larva like pupae?"

"Larva like ghost. Evil spirit. Romans used the word for the souls of the dead who come back to haunt the living. Look at the lovely gilt work! Some have crowns made of feathers. Piacere," she requested, and pointed.

The vendor promptly obliged.

"Now, this one's a bauta. See?" She traced the mask's contours. "It covers just your forehead to cheeks so you can still eat and drink. You'll see this one at Carnival. And such a funny nose: the shape changes the pitch of the wearer's voice. Women had to wear a bauta to go to the theater! And girls who weren't married couldn't."

"Why not?"

"So that lovers couldn't claim that they'd made a mistake. And," she smiled, "so trysting girls wouldn't put on this mask to slip away and lose their virginity."

Another aisle. Black velvet masks stared. "Moretta. Just for a woman, you hold it in place by clamping your teeth over this button. Terribly uncomfortable. She couldn't talk… makes a silent wearer even more mysterious, yes? Men wore a mask to throw eggs."

"To do what??"

"Throw eggs filled with rose water. They hurled them with a sling. Back in 1268 the Venetian council outlawed them. Too many nice clothes got ruined."

"Wow! That's got to be from one old fertility rite!" They both laughed, despite everything deeply and gladly in love, glad to be together in Venice.

"Oh, Lorrie. Everyone wore masks to gamble. Or visit whore houses. Historians think the masks started with the Romans' rites for purification and exorcism. I think the tradition is even older, way back to Dionysian rites of spring. For a while Carnevale stretched out for six months, can you imagine? It was brilliant. For a couple of weeks, masks made everyone feel equal. If you wore a mask, you were pardoned for any sins you committed. 'Anything goes', claimed a local saying."

"And later?"

"Well, there were two hundred quiet years."

The stretch of history in the city was beyond his comprehension. "Two hundred," Lorrie repeated dully.

The vendor mistook his comment for a request and Lorrie found himself holding a new mask.

"The Plague Doctor mask. A physician carried a stick, so he didn't have to touch his patients. The mask's long beak protected him from breathing in plague germs. I always think of carrion birds."

Hastily Lorrie handed back the beaky mask.

Suzanna happily continued her lecture, and for the first time Lorrie suspected Juliet had inherited a love of talking. "Italy revived Carnevale to push winter tourism. At masked balls everyone dresses up like the court of Louis XIV! You think you feel sleep-deprived now? Parties, parades, couples in matched masks and costumes striking poses, a bazillion tourists with telephoto lenses, people pushing to get pictures...."

☐

She stopped talking and turned to see what he was staring at

A masked spirit tilted its head as it listened to the history of Carnevale. The white and blue face tugged Suzanna's sleeve and she put her head close to the unmoving lips. "Go ahead," Suzanna said.

It transformed back to a girl and Juliet ran off in the direction of the nearest bridge.

"She wants to show off the mask to her friends. They all have masks, the less expensive ones, but you know girls... they love them. Wearing a mask turns them into something different."

"Someone?"

"No, some thing. They transform. Especially my girl. Juliet's a born actress."

Lorrie gingerly touched his scalp under the bandage. The swollen gash ached. "More like, a born soccer striker." Juliet had scored a direct hit; he just hoped his gift scored a point for his team. He looked over at the rows and rows of masks all staring from booths. "They're creepy," he blurted. "I'm not kidding. You know how some people feel about clowns? That's me with masks. Masks creep me out."

"Get used to them. Juliet and her clique would celebrate Carnevale all year if they could."

☐

The girls huddled, passing the new mask from hand to hand and comparing it to their own masks. Juliet dribbled Isabella's soccer ball and told them, "This morning I realized that my mom's friend didn't appreciate my *walking* tour. Half the time he wasn't even paying attention!"

"It's really Lorrie, and not Laura?" The idea of Juliet's mother loving other women like ages ago on that Greek island had titillated the girls. All were approaching puberty. All shared an intense curiosity and incomplete understanding of human biology.

Juliet set them straight. When she was old enough to understand, her mother had given her extremely clear explications about why she left Juliet's father. She explained what happens when husbands and partners sleep with other people. She wanted her daughter to understand the dangers of sex with strangers.

While she wanted her child to be aware of the perils lurking in sexual relations, Suzanna also wanted Juliet to know about the possibilities for intimacy and love. She informed the girl about homosexuality, and bisexuality, and the ways in which people love one another, physically or not. A year ago, her mother came home all smiles and talking in glowing terms about an old friend. Juliet had reached the obvious conclusion that the special friend was another girl.

Juliet's friends were disappointed that Lorrie was a he and not a she. As ringleader and reigning drama queen, she knew how to regain their attention. "When I first met him, he was asleep and didn't know it was me coming in the door. I didn't know he was there," she confided. "And, he was practically naked! He was under a blanket and it fell off when he stood up! I walked in the front door and girls, I screamed! He screamed too, and I started lobbing soda cans at him like each was a calcio. I nailed him good." The black and white soccer ball banged off a brick wall as she demonstrated.

"You *saw* him? Everything?"

"Almost," she qualified. "I felt bad, his head bled like a stuck pig. Though Mom says that's not a polite expression."

"Can we meet him?"

"They went back to pensione so he could take a nap.

Maybe he's up. Let's check!" The girls donned their masks and ran through the streets. Underneath Juliet's building, they huddled and looked up at the windows.

◻

Suzanna and Lorrie returned to the pensione and he went back to bed. He woke tangled in damp blankets as dusk began to fall. A sinking sun outside the tall windows hit the canal waters at the end of the block. Rays wobbled in ribbons of dying light.

A buzzer sounded out in the living room.

Lorrie went to the window. He pulled back the faded red velvet curtains and stepped out onto the tiny, narrow balcony. At the far end of the block he could see the sea. The shrinking arc of red sun dropped, the waters of Venice swallowing it whole.

He leaned over the scrolled railing, squinting; he could hear whispers, amplified in the alley. "Hey there! Hello?" His voice was far louder than he intended as it reverberated in the stone street.

A blue mask pointed in his direction. He rubbed his eyes: red, purple, royal blue, green, silver masks with ribbons waved at him. Voices shrieked as the figures parted and ran in the alleyway. *A coven of furies is stalking me,* he thought.

Suzanna spoke from the doorway. "I was just coming in to wake you up. Who in the world are you talking to?"

"You didn't hear the buzzer?"

"I was in the bathroom."

"Kids in masks have the apartment staked out."

"It must be Juliet and her friends."

"They were pointing at me!"

"Well, I could hear you calling *Hey there!* I'd be looking up this way, too." She looked more sharply at him. "Are you okay?" She came over and put a hand on his forehead.

"You're damp all over!" she exclaimed when she touched his back.

"I'm still groggy, I should have waited it out until bedtime. The jetlag," he qualified. "I'm fine, other than my eyes playing tricks."

"Come back to bed," she suggested, and pulled him back onto the sheets and blankets he had tangled into a ball as he napped.

☐

"He's dweeby," dark haired Chiara announced when the girls halted in Piazza San Polo. "Like Ichabod Crane. What a geek!" Chiara picked the perfect definer for the careful, thin Lorrie. Thanks to her American father and the steady supply of English-speaking films her family watched, Chiara's American slang was excellent.

"Tell us again. *Why* does he call himself Lorrie?" Maria demanded.

"He told Mom that his parents always said, Laurence James, before he got spanked when he was bad. Hearing his whole name meant a punishment was on the way. So, he made up his nickname."

"That's just weird," declared Donatella. "It's one thing to have a nickname. But, to change your name from a boy's name to a girl's?"

"Huh!" the girls agreed.

☐

Juliet sat in the living room when Lorrie and Suzanna came back out an hour later. She still wore the mask and its immobile expression made Lorrie unaccountably uncomfortable. He could swear that the staring mask knew that he and her mother had just made love; heck, it heard them. He thought, *There's no person behind it at all. It's just, the mask.*

"Hey Jules," Suzanna greeted, unconcerned. "How 'bout we go out for pizza?"

They took two lefts, a right, another two lefts, crossed a little bridge, and ended at a small pizzeria in a dead-end alley. Most of the guests spoke Italian.

"Ciao Suzanna!" the owner greeted them, pronouncing the name as Zoo sahn´ na. The two women exchanged air kisses and chatted in Italian; Lorrie stood and felt curiously adrift. Suzanna introduced him, and whatever Juliet in her mask added as she pointed in his direction made the pizzeria owner's eyes widen. The proprietress laughed, delighted. She gave a fast look under her eyelashes at his crotch. Smiling while she tsk-tsked and shook her head, she led them to the one normal-sized table in the room.

The mask remained over Juliet's face.

"Hungry?"

It nodded.

"Juliet," continued her mother calmly, "do you plan on not talking when you're wearing that?"

Nod.

"Well, then. Chicken, or green pasta?"

The mask bobbled.

"Sorry – was that yes to chicken?"

The mask moved back and forth.

"Green pasta?"

A vigorous nodding.

"Green pasta is pesto." Suzanna added, "This is a blessing in disguise. If Juliet's quiet for longer than fifteen minutes I usually call her doctor! This mask business is a *good* thing."

The mask thumped a foot on the floor to show displeasure, or agreement.

Lorrie ate the best pizza he had ever tasted. The crisp crust was perfect, just thick enough to hold the tomato sauce and buffalo mozzarella that melted away in his mouth. But he burned the skin on the inside of his cheek, hungry and too greedy with the smell of the cheese to wait before he bit into it.

"Lorrie knows someone famous," Suzanna announced.

Juliet removed her mask. "Really! Who?"

"Well, my second cousin Glen Timbrell." He threw Suzanna a look of gratitude for her help. A cousin was all he had to offer, painfully aware of how not interesting he himself was. "Glen's a stunt man."

Juliet perked up. "Any films I could watch? I bet Chiara has them!"

Lorrie obliged with the names of several blockbuster films, feeling proud by association.

Juliet's smile vanished. "Wait," she frowned, "if he's a stunt man, all you see is the back of his head. He has no face." She pulled the mask back down in disappointment.

*He has no face*, Lorrie repeated silently, and shivered.

Try how he might, that night he couldn't sleep. A blister throbbed inside his cheek where he had burned himself on the pizza. He doubled the dose of melatonin pills. They hadn't worked on the plane flights and weren't working now. At three in the morning he got up. Suzanna lay deep in dreams in the other twin bed.

He stepped onto the balcony. Lights flickered on the canal at the end of the alley. His vision swayed with unseen tides. Lorrie shivered in the night air. Watery images swam in the dim ghostly light reflected from the lagoon, blank eyes in immobile white faces, following his movements….

☐

The next day Suzanna purchased vaporetto passes for the boat to Murano. They made their way to the Rialto Mercado pier, Juliet in the middle, prancing in her mask.

On the vaporetto an Italian businessman tapped Lorrie's shoulder and wearily pointed to a prominent sign on the boat wall: a backpack with a slash through it. Lorrie removed the pack feeling foolish. His small daypack was hardly full and took up almost no space. All the tourists carried packs. None of them noticed the sign either. He perched in a bucket seat inside the cabin, unable to shut out the noisy, incomprehensible, polyglot conversations. The boat bobbed; his head hurt.

He went out on the open deck to join Juliet and Suzanna at the railing. "Is that Murano?" He pointed at a peaceful-looking island enclosed with a brick wall, behind which tall cypresses rose.

"Isola di San Michele. Cemetery," the mask informed him.

Lorrie quickly turned his gaze away.

He felt better as soon as they disembarked. Magnificent villas lined Murano's streets. In Venice, reflections on the canals lit the city. Murano glittered from the inside: bright glass filled every building. From cheap tourist baubles to ambitious hand-blown works of art, glass objects all sparkled and shone.

The shop doors opened to the warm Italian sunshine. Giant bunches of glass grapes hung from ceilings. Grapes glowed, lit from within. Incredulous, he made out the *veins* in the grape leaves.

They visited shops filled with sinuous twisting glass sculptures, or surreally real glass balloons. A shop specialized in large glass busts with surprisingly expressive faces. Other shops were filled with backlit shelves of large vases of glass ribbon candy.

*Even the Italians shine*, Lorrie thought enviously. They wore leather jackets, cashmere scarves, and perfectly buffed boots. Some of the men wore blue jeans, fitted and impeccably pressed. Lorrie looked over at Suzanna, as elegantly dressed as ever. Even Juliet in the eerie mask fit in far better than he did.

They stopped for a snack at an outdoor cafe. The edge of the canal was just a foot away from his chair. "Juliet, can we switch seats? The edge makes me nervous."

Luckily, the girl in the mask silently obliged him.

The high windows of a villa on the opposite side of the canal were all shuttered against the heat. Paint peeled in spots on the narrow balcony. Lorrie narrowed his eyes to see better: its flower boxes were filled with glittering green stems and colored petals made of glass. As decayed and shabby as it appeared, even with four hundred or five hundred or six hundred years of slow decline the Venetian region was a thousand times more glorious than anyplace he had ever been.

☐

They toured a massive glass blowing factory, now in its fifth generation. A burly man about Lorrie's age quietly entered the showroom, and they followed him into a spacious workshop in the back. A brick oven glowed with heat. The artisan wore a walrus mustache and glasses but no safety goggles. He wore a blue denim soft shirt over a tee shirt (the long sleeves perhaps a concession to safety), and a watch on his left wrist. He took a seat on a thick wooden bench. Old, well-used tools lined the seat; before it, a shop employee placed a metal bucket full of water. To the right was a small pit filled with finely ground glass.

"He's not even wearing safety gloves!" Lorrie whispered.

The man picked up a metal rod with a piece of glass at the end and stuck it briefly in the oven. He calmly twirled the molten glass; in seconds, a horse reared back. He twirled further and clipped the shape. A neck arched, nostrils flared, and the horse balanced on hind hooves. The glass blower set down his tools and left the room. The whole demonstration hadn't lasted longer than three minutes. *Three minutes.*

Given a different temperature the shapes would shift once again, outlines and contours flowing into one another. The miracle of Murano glass was that it continued melting.

Lorrie splurged on a traditional millefiori vase for Suzanna and the freshly made rearing equine figure for Juliet. When she hugged him thank you, the way the mask scraped across his shirt made him flinch.

□

For the trip back to Venice they boarded a slow vaporetto that stopped at every pier. Lorrie snapped picture after picture. Venice might be beautiful when one was on (relatively) solid ground. Seen from the water, the city was stunning. Their vaporetto floated by building after building decorated in elaborate mosaics outlining saints or marble staircases and moldings carved with disquieting winged lions. Lorrie glimpsed a marble arch and a wrought iron gate with wisteria climbing all over it.

Back at the pensione he uploaded everything onto his laptop. Juliet and Suzanna sat beside him on the couch and Lorrie started a slide show.

The photos were all out of focus. His pictures had streaks, as if the world were rushing by. Lorrie had tried to catch the waver of canal waters in the windows of the elegant buildings as they floated past. He had captured the water, but the reflections in windows were weirdly distorted. His own figure reflected, bent and wavering. *He was melting.* "That's a reflection on the water! I shouldn't look like I'm melting like a piece of Murano glass!"

The one solid figure in the photographs stood wearing a Venetian mask, implacable at the boat railing beside Lorrie as he melted.

That week they visited the oldest building in Venice, Piazza San Marco's Bell Tower. "Let's walk," Suzanna offered; Lorrie still wasn't sleeping. "The fresh air will do you good. Juliet's coming to meet us there after school."

They waited in a long line to get into the Bell Tower and in more lines for the elevator to the top. People kept staring. *XYZ? Examine your zipper?* Embarrassed, he wondered if his shorts were unzipped. Then he saw: the bruises on his legs from Juliet's attack had turned lurid shades of green and purple.

When they finally stepped out onto the roof, he kept a hand on the railings. Flocks of pigeons wheeled and circled, circled and wheeled. Statues around the tower perched to strike the hour or stared out to sea to inspect incoming ships. A proud lion raised its paw, claiming the region for Venice.

The piazza was so far below.

A snow-white tablecloth covered a tiny round metal table surrounded by four perfectly placed yellow seats. Next to it was a tiny round metal table covered by a snow-white tablecloth, surrounded by four perfectly placed yellow seats. Beside that one was a tiny round metal table covered by a snow-white tablecloth, surrounded by four perfectly placed yellow seats. Next to that one....

The sound of a saxophone climbed through the air. Lorrie followed the notes to a twin café on the other side of the piazza: yet more identical, tiny round metal tables, these covered with yellow tablecloths, the seats with rattan backs. Musicians in black tuxedos and bow ties played surprisingly good jazz.

He looked south. Wooden posts in rows lengthened and shortened in the waves. Rows of black gondolas floated, all covered with blue tarps. *How?* his tired brain kept repeating. *How can a city with all this chaos possess such perfect symmetry?*

When they got back to the square it was even more crowded. "Give me a second," he requested, and leaned against a lamppost and closed his eyes. When he reopened them, he was ringed by demons in Venetian masks. He shrieked.

A mask edged in blue jumped and grabbed Suzanna's hand. None of the jostling tourists even noticed.

Lorrie hung onto the post. "You and your friends scared the… Jeepers, Juliet! Don't do this to me!"

"Take your masks off, darlings?"

Juliet and her friends removed masks and all six stood silent.

"This is Chiara, and Isabella, and Maria, and Donatella, and Terry. Girls, shake hands with my friend Laurence Heples. Today you can call him Lorrie Helpless." Suzanna grinned at Lorrie and the children obediently moved forward to meet him.

No matter how hard he tried to control it, the arm he held out trembled.

"Lorrie, are you okay? You're a hot mess!" she exclaimed. "Let's get you back to the pensione. We're taking the next vaporetto."

He needed her help onto the boat. On the ride back, he clung to railings with his eyes closed. It was a little easier if he didn't see the waves.

☐

Sleep eluded him. In rare, feverish dreams he was pursued by Furies led by the Wicked Witch of the West. "I'm melting!" she screamed. "I'm melting!" Whenever he left the apartment Lorrie hunched, folding himself over double. Everything was terribly wrong.

Eight tortured days later he conceded defeat. "You know," he said hesitantly one afternoon, "I think I should leave. This was a big mistake."

"What do you mean, leave?"

"What were we thinking, having Juliet meet me here? Why didn't I wait, I shouldn't have been so anxious for us to form a family. What a laugh," he remarked, without a shred of humor. He pressed his thumbs into his eye sockets, seeking relief. "She doesn't like me. If I'd been smart, I would have waited for the two of you to move to Vermont. Maybe there Juliet wouldn't feel like I was poaching on her territory. Or that of her real father."

"*Biological* father," Suzanna said through clenched teeth.

"Biological. Right," he amended wearily. "Let's admit this was a mistake, okay? I'm going to change my ticket. I remember seeing a travel agency back near the train station area. A sign in the window said they speak English."

"How long have you been wanting to leave? Clearly this is something you've been thinking about. Planning."

"All I think about is how desperately I need to get some sleep. I can't plan anything; I can barely walk. Much less think straight! Look. How about I find out what my options are? And walk some. It would do me good to get fresh air and vitamin D."

"You'll only get lost." She shook his arm. "Lorrie, take a boat."

He fished a map of the Venetian streets out of his jacket pocket. "I bought this at the tabaccheria around the corner. I can always take a vaporetto if I can't find my way. God, I hate those canal boats." He clucked at his own foolishness. "Why didn't we wait until the fall? You'll be moving back before school starts."

"Just don't decide anything final." She began to cry. "You were my one true chance at a normal relationship," she wept. "After Giovanni I was sure I'd never find anybody. Who wants a partner with a precocious, hyper intelligent, highly-strung twelve-year-old? She never stops talking unless she's wearing a mask which she refuses to remove! Who in their right mind would be interested?"

"Me. *I'm* interested."

She sobbed.

For the first time in their courtship Lorrie saw how anxious she was. As Suzanna's mask slipped, he realized just how important their relationship was to her. And, he realized, to him. He put his arms around her and held her against his chest. She let her weight fall forward and he welcomed it. They stood like that, Lorrie gently stroking her hair, waiting for her to stop crying.

"Juliet's not a deal breaker?" She sniffled and tried to laugh; her voice quavered.

His ears rang with exhaustion. "I knew you were a single parent when we reconnected. It's nothing we can't figure out together." He kissed her quietly. "This isn't the place to do the figuring. We'll be better in America. We'll do better back on solid soil." Lorrie patted the map in his right pocket as if it were a life preserver. "Let me hear what the travel agency people say. We can plan for Vermont. It was stupid of me to think it would work right away. God, it was stupid." Lorrie gave her a last hug. He headed out the door and closed it gently behind him.

Suzanna went to the bathroom to wash her face. She began crying harder, tears dripping. Wide circles of smeared eyeliner and mascara rimmed her eyes; she looked like a raccoon. Or a tragedy mask, and not one worn at Carnevale. She dried her face and went back into the living room where Juliet was just coming in.

Juliet was in her mask.

"Close the door! And take that damned mask off!"

Juliet removed the mask but left the door ajar. "Mom? What's wrong?"

Suzanna crossed the room to close the door, slamming it hard. Juliet's arms flew through air and hit the table with the vase and the horse. The girl's reflexes were fast, and she grabbed the falling horse. Her mother let out a cry as the Murano vase smashed on the tiled floor. "You broke it!"

Juliet bit her lips. Her unmasked face scrunched. "That's the vase Lorrie bought, isn't it? Mom. I'm so sorry! It was so pretty!"

"Was." Suzanna's tears started again. "God, will I ever stop crying this afternoon?"

They knelt on the floor and picked up shards with their bare hands. Even the retrieved shards contained the lovely perfect forms of melting flowers and spreading starbursts of suns going nova.

Suzanna collected them into a saucer on the table. When she finished, she sat back on her heels. "We need to have a talk."

"I didn't do it on *purpose*," Juliet began. She stopped, fascinated by the expression on her mother's face. Suddenly worried, she plopped down on the couch.

"Lorrie wants to marry me. And, I want to marry him," Suzanna confessed. "We love one another, and he wants us to be a family. That's the real reason we're moving to Vermont. It was our mistake for not telling you all this right at the beginning."

"He's going to be my father?" Juliet's high-pitched voice rose another register.

"Stepfather," Suzanna sighed. "We thought, he could visit for a month so you could get to know each other. We didn't want to rush things or overwhelm you with the idea of Lorrie as your stepdad. We thought, let you meet him, get comfortable with the idea of having a man in our lives. When we go back to the US, you'll see where we'll live. He has the most wonderful place; his neighbors are farmers with apple orchards and they have a girl and boy about your age." She began to animate, as she tried to describe it. "They have ponies, you could finally learn to ride! You'll still come here to spend vacations with Nonna."

Juliet remained supernaturally still. "Will I have to call him Daddy?"

"You met him as Lorrie, I think you can go on calling him that." Suzanna began to feel hopeful.

"You really want to marry him? You don't think he's geeky?"

"Geeky? Oh, darling. Lorrie is totally geeky! That's one of the things I love about him, along with his honesty and sincerity and the way he really means anything he undertakes. *Yes*, I really want to marry him… and he just left for the train station." Her eyes leaked again. "He's at a travel agency, seeing about changing his ticket and leaving. He thinks you don't like him, and that it was a big mistake to come here. I am so scared! I'm afraid he'll fly right on out of here and decide it's not worth the trouble to be with a mother and child! Nothing about his visit with us has gone the way I wanted it to." Suzanna spotted a piece of glass behind a leg of the sofa. She bent to rescue its imploding blue and green novae.

It profoundly disturbed Juliet that this man who was so important to her mother did not want to be around her. She had never met an adult she couldn't charm. And her mother looked so sad again. Juliet was old enough to understand that her mother's previous nonstop sadness was not a good thing. Suzanna had been unhappy for years, fighting with Juliet's father and withdrawing into herself, withering. In the last months, Juliet sensed her mother slowly expanding, her contours filling out and replumping. "What do we do?"

"Number one, start talking again. Don't just sit there in your mask. Yes, you love it, and you can certainly wear it, but whether it's on or off you've got to talk with him. I know you and your silent treatment! I don't expect you to *adore* Lorrie. And I didn't expect that the first meeting would go smoothly all the time. Darling, the chance for us for a family depends on how the next few days go. I need you to make more of an effort. Can you do that for me?"

Juliet pictured herself and her mom, dressed in patchy rags, huddled against a stone wall of a side canal with a beggar's bowl in front of them. She cried as her fervid imagination went into overdrive. She saw Lorrie, his face a mask stony and unchanging as he dropped a pizza crust into the bowl. "Thank you, mister!" Juliet cried to his retreating figure. "Don't you have something for my mother?" Juliet cried harder. "I'll be nice! I promise, Mommy!"

She hadn't called Suzanna 'Mommy' in over a year.

Suzanna hugged her close. "We just need to let him know that we want him to stay, okay?"

Juliet clung to her. "I'll get my friends to help me look for him. We'll go meet his vaporetto."

"That's a great idea."

☐

On a boat heading back down the Grand Canal, Lorrie stood with his hands in his pockets. He fingered the edge of the tickets, reassured knowing they were there.

The buildings drifted by as he felt *himself* melt and flow. This was what he had come to Italy for, really. His life needed less rigidity; it needed to open to love and a more fluid structure. So what, if this unnerving dreamy city was where he'd landed? So what, if the structures had been built on posts in shivering fluids? It was reality, and reality shifts and flows.

He thought and thought as the vaporetto moved through the canal.

*What was he doing? Maybe I'll stay, and we can work things out after all? What's so hard about figuring out how to make friends with an adolescent girl?* Lorrie got out at the next vaporetto stop and ran back to the travel office. "I changed my mind!" he announced.

The agents groaned and shrugged. Tourists!

Twenty minutes later Lorrie was on a boat heading head back to the two females who were his family now. For the first time, he felt comfortable riding on a boat. The vaporetto's movement lulled him. Instead of wanting to throw up, he was newborn. He was a figurative infant, Moses in a cradle, the boat rocking him gently.

Lorrie slept soundly past the next five piers.

He woke at Ca' Rezzonico, got off the boat - and immediately lost his bearings. Wasn't *that* the corner cafeteria with a shop with tourist trinkets next door? Tour groups and people with backpacks and rolling suitcases rumbled across the bridges. Lorrie fought through the crowds as his anxiety returned. It was irrational, really. How could you be claustrophobic in a place with open water all around?

He took out his map and tried to remember where he had disembarked. According to the map the vaporetto stop he wanted was on the opposite shore. Belatedly he recalled that the vaporetto boats served both sides of the canal. *Great God,* he thought, exasperated that he had gotten lost yet again.

After fifteen minutes of backtracking he saw an arrow pointing to the Rialto Mercado stop. Lorrie stepped out onto the boat landing. Incredibly, it was deserted save for a family of ducks swimming alongside the canal wall. *Check one last time,* he thought, and bent his head back over the diagram with its deceptively simple looking street layout. The map really was a lifesaver.

The call of a siren carried over the waters and swam through his thoughts. A yellow water ambulance cut through the Grand Canal. Boats pulled out of its way to give the pilot more room to navigate; the ambulance never slowed. Waves crested out from both sides.

A vaporetto approached in the opposite direction, aiming for the pier.

*Quack Quack*

A Scottish tour group, the leader holding a plaid umbrella high in the air, crowded onto the landing and Lorrie was alone no longer. A family in green tams shoved closer. All four children wore large silver thistle pins. Russet curls bobbed under their tams and their bright blue eyes stared into Lorrie's.

The ambulance screamed, about to arrive. The blue light flashed as the smallest child shrank back, frightened by the wail of the siren.

The children's father waved his arms. "Laura! Move away from the water!" He shouted as the siren blared. "Come to me! Come to Papa!" The children pushed to get past Lorrie, everyone dangerously close to the edge of the pier.

A group of girls wearing masks suddenly appeared. They wheeled like sea gulls when they saw him. Lorrie took an involuntary step back. The masks ran faster, shrieking something he couldn't hear. The water ambulance pulled up, now parallel to the docking vaporetto.

A mask edged in blue threw out its arms for a wide hug. "Laurence James!"

The family of ducks scrambled onto the pier, all of them quacking angrily. The birds were as trapped as he was. Lorrie felt a searing pain at his instep as a mallard pecked angrily. The mallard's mate pecked at him, too. He tried to step over the ducks as tourists with daypacks jostled him from behind.

"Come to Papa now!" the Scot shouted.

Lorrie dropped his map and it fluttered in an updraft and landed out on the water. The ambulance plowed over it. Lorrie turned, and the group of masks descended. "Laurence James!" they yelled as the girls rushed towards him.

The currents moved, and, as they always do, objects in the eternal canals smeared and melted. Tourists, staring from the arriving boat, were the last solid figures Lorrie saw before he vanished in the water.

# BETTER WEATHER

I saw it coming. A hurricane doesn't sneak onto land; meteorologists had carefully tracked the growing storm and predicted its arrival. Businesses, hospitals, and schools had closed, residents ordered to evacuate the designated danger areas.

I had every warning I needed and should have prepared myself for approaching disaster. And yet, it caught me. I discovered the hard way it's not just weather systems that bring danger. What really destroy you are the emotional storms. When my storm arrived, I was trapped in my home with no place to escape to and no way to deflect its force.

As a married woman I felt safe; I felt anchored. With Travis by my side I'd finally beaten the odds. I thought we would be together forever. But, on the day before the hurricane hit, I came home to a silent house. Travis was gone and a sealed envelope lay on the kitchen counter. I had a feeling of foreboding as I opened it, but I still didn't know.

From the looks of it, Travis had scribbled the message in a hurry. *"Those men looking for you came back. You promised you'd stop gambling, but you didn't. You lied. You never stop lying,"* his note said. *"I'm done, Sheila, can you understand? The hurricane might take the house. One way or another, either this storm or your gambling could get you killed, and I can't watch. I'm gone, and you need to go too. Start a new life somewhere else. Run, before it's too late."* And just like that, like the ponies I bet on that hadn't played out, my life went off track. Until today I had been able to avoid the fallout from my mistakes, so how did I miss the signs that Travis was leaving me?

The hurricane arrived the next morning when I was re-

reading his letter. Rain gusted across the yard and spattered the house. The storm grew, lashing the windowpanes in waves. While a Category Five hurricane battered my city, I stayed hunched over the documents I had spread out on the table. The answers to what had gone wrong was in them somewhere.

My black notebook. The lists started in clear handwriting, but the final pages were terrible scrawled columns of numbers. Legal papers, including a petition for divorce (yet another surprise; I didn't even know Travis had a lawyer). And a notice from our bank, informing me that my loving husband had removed his name from our joint account. Funds transferred; Travis had quietly removed his share of the money while I was preoccupied with not getting hurt.

A predicted major storm can be a comfort if all you know are continuing random disasters. Yes, I assure you, the howl of the winds was a comfort. The storm's rhythm was oddly calming. It was the Universe blowing in and out, in and out.

I looked up from my reading and cocked my head. The winds now screeched. Rain hammered on the roof tiles. And then, a signal from another planet, my cell phone rang. Unknown caller: the caller was probably the loan sharks. *Just you wait till the storm's over,* I imagined them telling me.

I let it ring ten times before I picked it up. "Hello?"

"Sheila?"

I recognized his voice despite the din. "Travis!" In a spate of anger last night, I'd removed his name from my list of contacts. And, despite that anger, I was instantly hopeful again. We gamblers are compulsive optimists.

"Is that rain I hear?"

"Yeah, I'm at the house. Maybe you forgot I've got documents to sign."

"You're still there? Get out! The hurricane's coming!"

"It's already here." My voice was calm. I held out my free palm and was pleased to see my hand didn't tremble. "It's already here," I repeated. "You left me quite the disaster." And with a last, abrupt whoop, the winds died.

My husband's voice in my ear was suddenly loud. "Sheila? What just happened? Why'd it just get so quiet?"

"The eye of the storm might be right overhead, I think."

"You fool, now there's no way out! You'll be caught right in the middle of it!"

"Oh, Travis. No. No, no, no. Actually, I'm caught in the middle of our living room." I looked around, trying to see the room in detail. I noticed only was what was missing: my husband. "I told you. I'm going through legal papers. Hey, I locked all the doors and I even filled the tub last night. They say you should fill receptacles with water if you're stuck in a natural disaster. Isn't that funny? A hundred to one odds this storm brings more water than I'll ever drink."

"Sheila." His voice was quiet. "Do something for me, okay? Get the flashlight and take your cell phone. This storm is incredibly dangerous. You need to go down in the cellar."

So, I did what I always do when he makes a suggestion: the exact opposite. I opened the front door and stepped out onto the porch. Water dripped and drained, but otherwise the yard was still. "Travis, it's totally peaceful. Clear blue skies! Not a cloud in sight!" And this was true for a patch of the skies directly above my head: a cloudless, clear hole. It was like standing in the middle of the planet's largest stadium. The eyewall of the storm was a funnel with mile-high sides constructed from gray cloud banks. They spiraled counterclockwise and massed in the heavens, as far as I could see. Moist, heated air twisted up and up and up and up.

"It's hot here," I said absently. My skin was damp, not just from stress and the water drenching everything, but because it was so warm. I took a step and stumbled, then grabbed for a porch post as my vision blurred. "Woah. I feel dizzy."

"In the storm eye, barometric pressure drops, Sheila. It's

messing with your blood pressure. For God's sake, get in the cellar."

All at once I was more frightened than I'd ever been in my life. "I'm going to the cellar now," I told Travis. "Keep talking, okay?" I hung on to the sound of his voice and went back indoors. It was hard to navigate the cellar steps, but I managed it by gripping the railing.

"You're in the cellar?"

"Yeah, I'm in it. Dead center." I turned on the lights. "Or is it that I'm in the center, dead? Katrina, Irma, Harvey, and now this one. None of the others can match it. Hurricane Travis, Category Off the Charts. I'll call you back." I hung up. I stood without moving a muscle. When my head finally felt clear, I climbed the cellar stairs to fetch what I would need.

I screamed when I caught sight of the harridan in the hallway mirror. Eyes that were too large stared back at me from a pale face. The hair that framed my reflection stood on end, the strands radiating out in a demonic halo. "Static electricity," I said aloud, and for luck I repeated the phrase. I shook my head at the apparition and, not wanting to see her, went back to the cellar. Ceremoniously I placed candles, matches, booze, gallon jugs of water, cans and a can opener on the cellar work bench.

Gradually the other side of the cellar came into focus. *Warm clothes*, I reminded myself, and I fetched my sweatshirts from the top of the dryer where I had folded them in a stack a week ago. Another trip upstairs for pillows and blankets. I could tell the eye of the storm had passed because rain started lashing the windowpanes again. I ignored the rising moan of the wind and took my burdens with me.

I made a final trip up those stairs for the documents. The seriousness of my situation returned, cold and heavy as gravity, as the barometric pressure rose back up. I fancied I could see the electrons of dust motes swirling in the cellar air.

But I was more alert, and this time when my cell phone buzzed I answered on the first ring.

"Travis?"

"No, this is the people you owe a lot of money, Mrs. Green. You'll be seeing us sooner than you think."

I started to laugh; I couldn't help myself. "In the middle of a Category Five storm? Are you people for real? Come and get me," I said, and hung up. The storm became more violent and twenty minutes later something banged insistent on the walls, then the door. Was it the hurricane or a visitor? I heard glass shatter as the windows in a room upstairs imploded.

Ah, the Wheel of Fortune spins and whirls. At its center is a cosmic eye that sees all, knows all, and weighs all. It measures our flaws, our misguided belief in second chances, and third chances, and fourth chances, and winning streaks, and races that aren't rigged. A storm had swallowed me whole. I had gone through its monster belly, and it was about to spit me back out.

God's fists renewed their banging on my home and I listened as the tiles on the roof stripped, broke, and flew away. The door at the top of the cellar stairs blew open as the lights went out.

I stayed in the chair despite my heart's wild thumping to escape. I sat erect and straight, even as I twisted in knots of fear. I lit the candles; I made a bet with myself about how many minutes it would take before my hands really began to tremble.

"Come on down," I said.

# RULES TO LIVE BY

"You don't like them? Then why don't you ask your father for his suggestions?" Nicole looked at Danny.

Danny set aside the school assignment she needed to finish. "Daddy told me to ask you." She tugged blond hair over her eyes, hiding her face. Then she flipped her head back, enjoying the way her hair flew through the air before settling on her shoulders. She waited in case her mother had more to say. When Nicole didn't add anything, Danny asked, "Mom, are you *sure* these are what I need?"

"Not right now, but they'll serve you your whole life." Nicole nodded her head in agreement with her own words.

"But are these serious or just for fun? How can I even tell?"

"That's up to you. It's always good to keep a few classic pointers in mind. At nine and a half years old, you're not too young to learn these things. *Especially* at a young age!"

"Isn't all this reto… retro…."

"Retroactive," her mother supplied the term. "And, no. It's not. I *do* want you and your brother and sister to get college educations or learn a trade. Even better, both, if that's what you want. I *do* want you to know that you can be anything you want, honey, anything, and that includes President of the United States and Chairwoman of the Board. When you get there, though, you'll need to know some other things too."

Danny rolled her eyes. "Like Daddy says, are you in one of those moods? Or did you guys have a fight?"

"I want to spare you some of my mistakes," her mother dodged. "And your father's out enjoying his God-given right to go play golf."

"You hate golf! You think it's boring."

"Finish your homework," said Nicole. "And good grief, when did you get so smart? You don't need any advice from the experts." Nicole bent over and kissed Danny's shiny head. Her daughter didn't respond. Nicole couldn't see her expression. Danny had her head lowered with her hair back over her face, and she was scoring the schoolwork assignment with fierce lines of red pen.

"All that beautiful hair!" Nicole marveled, smiling as she left Danny's bedroom. The smile vanished once she was out in the hallway. Her eyes took in the mess on the floor. Nicole stepped over discarded jackets, book bags, the groceries she hadn't put away yet. Taffy had coughed up fur balls in the corner again. "Clean house on the weekend when there's golf to be played? Life, as lived by Mrs. Gleason," she murmured.

☐

The lasagna Nicole set on the table two nights later was perfect, but Rich was still settling Louie into his highchair. Theresa wore headphones and didn't hear her mother call her to dinner. Danny was out walking the family dog. By the time everyone washed their hands, the girls took their seats, the cat and the dog had been fed and all electronic gadgets turned off, the meal was cold. "Just once it would be nice to have everyone seated the first time I call you to dinner," Nicole stated quietly as her family passed dishes around the table. "Just once!" And that was when the house phone rang.

Rich set aside the plate of food he was cutting into bites for Louie. "Hello? Yes, this is Mr. Gleason. Who's calling?" Rich talked on for a few minutes and waved to Nicole to take the phone. He put a palm over the receiver. "It's Danny's teacher. She wants to talk with both of us, but you in particular," he said, and held the phone out to his wife.

Nicole raised her eyebrows at Danny, who shrugged. "Mrs. Herbert? This is Danielle's mother Nicole."

"Hi Nicole, Janet Herbert here. I apologize for calling during dinner," the teacher said. "But Class Night is next week and I'm calling to encourage all our parents to attend. We're hoping to do some parent-teacher conferencing at the same time. Strictly informal. I'd like a few minutes to talk about Danielle and how things are going at home," she continued.

"How things are going at home? Things, at home, are going fine. Is there a problem with things at school we should know about?"

"No problem at all, but I'd appreciate it if you could give me five minutes after the presentations."

"Thursday night then," Nicole agreed.

Rich returned to dishing food onto Louie's plate. "Why did Mrs. Herbert only want to talk to you? She's got to know both of us always sign up to go to Class Night."

"Hard to say. Her tone was disturbingly neutral."

"And what's this about a problem with Danny? Did she say something about trouble?" asked her husband.

"Well, Mrs. Herbert says," Nicole began, but Danny's mouth opened in protest.

"I don't have any problems at school!" she wailed. Her lips quivered; she was ready to burst into tears.

"Of course you don't, honey. Mrs. Herbert wants to talk with me individually for a few minutes. She probably wants to ask me to come in and talk to your class on Careers Day. You know, mom as manager of an animal shelter and all that."

Rich tickled Louie to get him to laugh and aimed a fork of food at his mouth. "Well, if Danny's been up to no good," (he waggled his ears and all three kids giggled), "we'll find out about it sooner or later. Okay people, let's eat!"

Class Night was intended as an opportunity for dads and moms to see their children's schoolwork without the usual pressures. Parents had no need to weigh or discuss; this was a time to admire what their offspring had learned and created that year. The children themselves were at home, parked in front of televisions or playing computer games.

The room was crowded, the voices loud. Forty parents stood in small groups in the elementary schoolroom, talking with other moms and dads. For an occasion ostensibly 'just to take a look' at their offspring's schoolwork, some parents felt anxious. Most of them secretly worried how their child measured up to the other kids.

Not Rich: he moved around the classroom by Nicole's side without a care in the world. Rich loved Theresa and Louie and Danny just as they were. "Stop looking so uptight," he told his wife. "If our kids don't grow up to be axe murderers or politicians, we'll have succeeded at our jobs. Danny's a good kid. Hey – is that her mask?"

In honor of Class Night, the children molded papier-mâché masks of themselves. Gestalts, some solemn, some with happy faces, gazed upon the adults. Danny's mask hung at adult eye level on the back wall. "She sure has your nose, babe," Rich remarked. "But didn't their art teacher tell them to smile? Her mask looks sad. When did kids get so serious? And look at these! Good God, a gift supplies store must have exploded in here!" He grinned and indicated other art projects, heavy with clumps of silver and gold glitter embedded in thick white paste. Yet more decorative glitter winked out from drawings and watercolor paintings.

Hand-made mobiles swayed over the desks. These depicted figures of who the children wanted to be when they grew up, or items important in their lives. Friends, favorite pets, and toys dangled, currently tangle-free. Fire fighters and ballet dancers fluttered hopefully, but rappers and explorers and a president hung there as well. Other mobiles, made from strips of heavy paper, spelled out phrases. Adverbs, possessive pronouns, adjectives, and action verbs swirled in crosscurrents created by the adults moving about the room. Taped to each desk was the name of the child who chose those defining tags.

Rich walked by the desk to the left of Danny's. Above his head swayed the phrase *Scared - run - faster!* and the words *weather (noun) – Heather (proper noun) – clever (adj)*.

A folder of oversized, extra-heavy construction paper lay on Danny's desk, filled with her stories and finished tests. He squashed his big body in her seat and scanned Danny's work; it was of fine quality. Mrs. Herbert had written *Danny's solid B average showed a good steady mind and a willingness to finish each piece.* Rich was thoughtful as he slowly leafed through her assignments and tests. "Her work's a hundred times better than what I brought home at this age," he commented.

Rich stood back up and the top of his head brushed his daughter's mobile. *Fight –secrets - forgive. Mommy – Daddy - kiss.* "Where's that class project she was working on?"

"Up in the front." Nicole pointed to the blackboard behind Mrs. Herbert's desk. Large block letters filled the blackboard. In alternating blue and green chalk, it asked *SERIOUS OR JUST FOR FUN? RULES TO LIVE BY from MRS. HERBERT'S FOURTH GRADE, ROOM B.* A table below the blackboard was invisible under large colored sheets.

They headed over for a look, but other parents already waited in line. Bart and Kiara Jackson, the parents of Danny's friend Amber bent over the pages, laughing. They straightened when they spotted Nicole and tried to look serious. Bart Jackson gave her a fleeting look and ran a hand over his neatly trimmed afro. "Hey Rich, that's some advice for fourth graders Nick's got in there."

"Bartholomew!" chided Kiara. "Nicole, Rich, nice to see you." Kiara tugged on Bart's arm and drew him away.

"What was that all about?" asked Rich.

Nicole smiled gaily, trying to look innocent. "Got me."

☐

The Gleasons waited for their turn to look through the pages. When they reached the table, they began to read sheets of construction paper, all hand-lettered and decorated with pictures, aloud to one another.

"Here's Amber's," Nicole reported. "It says: My parents tell me, 1. Speak truth to power. 2. There is more to life than good hair. 3 Read at least one book a week." A rainbow decorated the top of her yellow page. Amber had drawn smiling black girls wearing braids that hung to their waists, all the girls connected with strings of little pink hearts.

Rich read the next class project. "Arthur Gill's. My parents remind me to 1. Always eat your vegetables. 2. Even the president can begin somewhere small and humble. 3. You get what you earn. Check out Art's decorations." Art had filled his borders with space explorers in round helmets and see-through rockets. They fired orange and yellow flames out the back as they blasted off into the cosmos. "Is there a genetic difference between little boys and girls? *Yes*, there's a genetic difference between little boys and girls." Rich pointed to the astronauts as proof.

"You've got that right. There's lots of truth in your words, Mr. Gleason," Danny's teacher agreed as she walked over. Mrs. Herbert had pulled her frosted blond hair back in a ponytail. She wore a suit and heels for the evening, and the outfit underscored the authority she exuded. "Boys express and project themselves into the world around them in markedly different ways from how girls do. Although," eyes hooded, Mrs. Herbert looked pointedly at Nicole, "children get most of how they perceive the world from their parents. Keep reading, I believe you're about to come across Danielle's page." Casually the teacher crossed her arms and waited.

Rich was only half-listening as he turned more project pages and read aloud; he was having too much fun. "Sherry Jennings: 1. Science is the art of observing the world around us. 2. Animals are our friends. 3. You catch more flies with honey than with vinegar. Now, this girl is definitely a future scientist. Check this out," he said happily. The page was bedecked with rows of precisely drawn ladybugs. Every second bug had four black spots on her red carapace; on the others, five. Rich set Sherry Jennings's page aside and handed Nicole the next one to read.

"1. Never, ever lie about anything except your golf scores. 2. Business may be cutthroat, but you don't have to be. 3. The most important rule of all: Don't forget to brush your teeth. These are from the Whalen boy."

"He must have gotten them from what's his face, his old man Herb," said Rich.

"Including the last rule," commented Nicole, recalling a boy with constant halitosis from recent children's birthday parties. Herb Whalen was trying to make sure his son followed in his footsteps, with limited success.

"These are terrific!" Rich declared. "What did you tell Danny to write?"

"Don't take it too seriously, Rich," Nicole cautioned, her cheeks flushing bright red. Nicole pretended not to see the teacher who remained standing next to her, within earshot.

"Here's Danny's!"

Mrs. Herbert moved closer.

With a flourish Rich spread their daughter's page out on the top of the pile. He scanned it and paused; the wrinkles on his forehead stood out. "She didn't do a drawing. And you gave her these as rules to live by?" In a carefully measured tone he read aloud, "Danielle Gleason. My mother's advice is: 1. Jewelry always fits. 2. Get an education, or the world might give you one you didn't bargain for. 3. Never marry a man with a behind smaller than your own. That way yours will always look good." Very, very slowly he put down Danny's page. "Jesus Christ, Nick," he hissed. "What the *hell* were you thinking?"

"You took off to play golf that day," his wife hissed back, as if that fact explained everything. A parent she didn't know tapped Mrs. Herbert on the elbow. Reluctant, the teacher had to turn and move away. Nicole was relieved. She prepared to defend herself, but Rich was no longer paying attention.

Her husband was attempting to look over his shoulder at his own behind. He turned back and glanced at his crotch. With a thoughtful expression he looked Nicole over, examining her from her feet to her head and back again. "Never thought about the business with the butt," Rich said in an absent tone, and he craned his neck back over his own shoulder. "I have to admit, it's true, I'll give you that!" He began to laugh. "Here comes a case in point."

The Merriweathers approached the table. Mrs. Merriweather lifted weights four nights a week; she had a magnificent washboard stomach and thunder thighs. Her healthy aura sucked away all the air around her slender husband. Mr. Merriweather had the ungainly appearance of a nervous man who smoked too much. He wore slacks, and the thin material made his skinny legs appear even thinner.

Nicole and Rich looked away from the Merriweather thighs and into their faces. "Helen, Roger," Rich greeted them.

"You look serious, Rich," boomed Helen.

The Gleason couple burst into laughter. "Not at all, Helen, not at all," Rich finally got out. He wiped his eyes and gave his wife a surreptitious pat on the behind. "Let's go, sweet thing," he said with a private smile.

"Honestly, some people," Roger murmured as Danny's parents moved away. "Here's Robby's page! Listen: 1. A healthy mind in a healthy body. 2. Discipline is your friend. 3. Keep up the good work and...." A crayoned little boy wore a frown and attempted weights far too heavy for him.

*Fat, slow, ugly. Wit hit sit. Sadly badly madly. Yours theirs mine.* Words eddied in hidden, secret currents, always in movement. *Rite write right. Cot caught. Lay ley lei lie lye.* Mrs. Herbert's class studied synonyms and homonyms and wrote them up.

Unwatched, unnoticed by the parents, dangling on strings above their heads, labels swirled.

What the air contains, children learn.

# The River

"Why aren't you out playing?"

"It's cold Daddy; it's still snowing."

"On days like this, if the sun keeps shining you think it can't ever be cold. There may be snow in the woods and deep on the ground, but the sunlight sparkling in the ice crystals is dazzling. When I was a little boy about your age, in wintertime I liked to go for walks and think up stories."

"I'd still rather be inside by the fire. Tell *me* a story?"

"Ok, how about I tell you a Winter's Tale, something just for this time of year? Would you like a made-up story, or a real story?"

"Oh, real, please! Tell me a real one!"

"Almost every detail will be true. I promise. This is the story of my grandmother and her papa."

"Did they die a long time ago?"

"Well, my grandmother is dead. But as for her papa? No one knows."

"You mean he's alive somewhere? That's silly!"

"Shh. Sit closer to the fire, and I'll tell you the story…. This story is called, let's see: The River."

### The River

My grandmama's name was Margaretha, but everyone called her Gretel, just like the girl in the fairytale about Hansel and Gretel. She grew up in a faraway country that you can't find on the maps anymore. Her family lived on the Danube River. And where they lived was part of the Austro-Hungarian Empire, a big kingdom that used to stretch all the way from the Black Forest almost to the Black Sea.

"Was Gretel a princess?"

"No."

Her ancestors didn't have enough to eat in winters as cold as this one, and so the king moved them to the southern part of his empire where they could build houses to stay warm, and farm the land, and always have enough food. Around them were towns that only spoke Serbian, they were like an island of German speakers in a country of Slavs. She had one brother, a little sister, and an aunt. Gretel's parents were Eva and Ludwig.

"Your great grandpapa?"

"Yes. That very one."

He was born on December 31st, the last day of the year, over one hundred years ago. Like I say, Ludwig had three children, but Gretel was his favorite. He loved her more than anything. Whenever he went to Belgrade for business, he always brought her presents. Sometimes he brought candy from a big Belgrade department store. Oh, Gretel loved sweets! And he brought her a doll with real hair, and with eyes that opened and closed. "I'll call her Agnes," Gretel decided. Gretel was the most popular girl in school after that! Everyone wanted to be her best friend and play with that doll! Her mother sewed it a dirndl. And the next-door neighbor was a tinsmith and he made a tin wagon and painted it red, just for Gretel's dolly.

Their house was in the town, and Ludwig worked the land by the river that had belonged to his parents. They grew apples, and pears with fruit as red as blood, and peaches, and red and white grapes for wine and to make a strong liquor, the kind that burned your lips going down and started a glowing fire inside your belly. They had fields of wheat and oats, corn, and barley. They saved the corn cobs and burned them in the oven, to heat water in a big wooden tub for the baths they took once a week. Gretel and her brother each had their own rooms and her baby sister slept in a crib, and there was even a room for Gretel's aunt.

Their neighbors were Catholic or Orthodox or Protestant, and the tailor in town was Jewish. His name was Mr. Klopfer and he helped everyone with their trousseau, which is the clothes, and sheets, and table linens a married couple needs when they first set up house.

Gretel would go with her papa to check if the grapes growing along the riverbanks were ripe. Twice a year everyone was let out of school early, to bring in the harvests and when it was time to slaughter the pigs and make ham and bacon and sausage. Her family lived on the one big street that ran through the town. Gretel helped sweep it when the queen of Yugoslavia came to the area. But on most days only one car a day drove through.

Gretel's family had a radio, in the living room. One of their neighbors knew that something called a television had been invented. It's a box, he claimed, and you push a button and you can see pictures as well as hear. No one believed him.

"No one there had a tv?"

"Nope! No one had even seen a tv. Still, that town was the best, most perfect place, and they had the best lives, my grandmama always told me."

Everybody got along. But it didn't stay that way…. Because a war came to Europe. With time the war reached all the way to the little town. The older boys had to join the army. Most of them had never left the area and still they had to go fight. It got worse; the neighbors turned on one another. The townspeople turned on the Jewish family. They marched to the tailor's shop and threw bricks through the windows. Then they climbed over the broken glass, entered the shop, and stole the bolts of cloth and sewing machines and carried them away. Gretel and her brother stood and watched as his friends helped rob the shop. It didn't matter that they had played soccer with Mr. Klopfer's son just the week before.

One day, officers of the German Air Force, the Luftwaffe came. Her mother said, "Gretel, you're going to sleep in your aunt's room from now on." And Ludwig hid the radio because the officers would have taken it away from them.

The officers moved into the house and they stayed for months. "You're such a hardworking little girl," they told Gretel. They said, "It's so clean and tidy here! After the Saturday sweeping and cleaning, we can walk through the streets with just our socks on and they don't get dirty! This town is the first place we'll come for vacation when the war is over."

But the war went on, and as the front came closer the soldiers and officers left for new battlefields. The family could listen to the radio again; Papa took the radio out of its hiding place. The news reports told them secrets. An announcer's voice listed the numbers of soldiers who were dead and told them about the battles that the government kept out of the official news reports.

Then came the scariest day of Gretel's life.

On that day, someone banged with hard thuds on the door. Gretel stood behind her father as he opened it. A group of men holding hunting rifles and heavy sticks stood on the porch. "Germany has lost the war. You have two hours."

"Two hours for what?" Gretel asked, but no one paid attention.

"Get the wagon," Papa told her brother. Her parents piled the wagon with meats from the smoke house, and bushel bags of potatoes and corn, and filled a basket with vegetables. Mama and Papa had put on layers and layers of clothes, even though it was summertime.

"Get your boots and your winter coat, Gretel," Mama ordered. Her brother hitched one of the horses to the wagon while Papa led the second horse out by its bridle.

*The River*

The Serbs stared with hard eyes. They didn't even wait until the wagon turned into the street before they entered the house. A man came back onto the porch; he held the radio in one hand and Agnes in the other. In the rush to pack, Gretel had forgotten her doll. "We have to rescue Agnes!" she said and began to climb out of the wagon.

Her brother grabbed the hem of her coat and pulled Gretel through the air to his side. "Why can't I bring Agnes?" Gretel wailed. Mama crouched with her elbows over her hair. Ludwig rode alongside the wagon without saying a word.

They drove up the road, heading north.

The broad street was now filled with families seeking a route away from revenge and retribution. It didn't matter that they had lived in the town all their lives, and generations before them, all of their parents and grandparents and great-grandparents. They had to leave. An hour later Mama lay on her side in the bottom of the wagon, still crying. Her coat hid her head, but her body shook. Gretel's aunt slumped in a corner, holding tight to Gretel's little sister. From the front where she sat beside her brother, Gretel stared at a caravan of people she had known her whole life. In the road all around them came even more people, pushing full barrows and carrying lumpy bundles. Ludwig's mouth was a grim tight slash in his face. He rode close beside the wagon, and still didn't speak.

Abruptly, suddenly, Ludwig clucked to his horse and pulled on the reins. He turned in a circle, back towards the way they had come. "I have to go back and take care of something. I'll meet you at the border." He guided his mount over to the side of the road and into a field. Moving swiftly now, he rode away.

"Where's the border?" asked Gretel. She couldn't stop feeling anxious, like how you feel in a bad dream where you can't wake up.

"A couple of hours away. I think." Her brother glanced at

her face. "Don't worry, Gretel. We'll wait for him. Papa will meet us there."

Gretel twisted on the wooden seat. As far as she could see, a slow parade rolled northward with only her father moving against the tide. Papa and his horse grew smaller and smaller, and vanished.

Gretel and her family reached the border and waited. They waited for days. More and more frightened people joined them, but Ludwig didn't come. Finally, they had to leave. The stream of refugees had grown into a river, and then a flood, and become a huge tide of history and fate sweeping them up and away. They travelled first to Austria, and on to Hessen. Everywhere they went they asked for news of Ludwig and left messages for him. In Hessen, just Gretel alone was taken in by a butcher's family. She had to work awfully hard but she was lucky: she always had food.

No one ever saw Ludwig again. He never returned, and to this day my great grandpapa is listed as *Missing*. He doesn't have a death certificate and there are no dates for his grave.

"That, my darling boy, is the tale of Gretel and her papa Ludwig. She never stopped missing him."

"But Daddy, is that the end to the story?"

"Yes and no. When I was your age and would go on walks in the winter as it grew dark, I tried to imagine what happened to him. Maybe Ludwig rode back to help others pack their belongings so they could leave. Or he was killed as an enemy, a German. Or someone stole his horse. Or he joined an army in a foolish, final, quixotic burst of patriotism. Or maybe, just maybe, he rode as far as he could in another direction, a different one. Maybe he discovered a route far away from all the people making war or escaping war. He rode off to a place where he could start over, and neighbors live in peace together, and he waits there for this world to end and the next one to begin, a place where he and Gretel and all the others are waiting for us to join them. No one knows what happened to him. But I like to imagine that maybe he went someplace different and better. And when he got there, they all lived, happily ever after."

The End.

*Dedicated to the memory of my mother-in-law Margaretha Reder Hartmann, the real-life Gretel of this story*

# WHAT DIED IN THE FRIDGE

One sweet Wednesday afternoon, on a Halloween some years ago, Eddie Cooper and Clint York dropped acid. Was it a wish to get closer to God, to step through Huxley's doors of perception, to follow in the footsteps of the bands they loved? Were Eddie and Clint taking a university course called History of Great Thinkers and exploring Plato's allegories about how to perceive true reality?

Could it be because enlightenment doesn't care how you get there?

No.

Eddie and Clint were high school seniors, not college students, and *The Wizard of Oz* was on cable television that night. *The Wizard of Oz* is a movie made for hallucinogens, perfect for a first, initiatory acid trip. Clint had mentioned the idea and Eddie agreed at once. Eddie's older brother Kyle had tripped, and he was still around.

Just once, they thought. What could go wrong? They plotted out the experiential stages of the drug and calculated when to ingest the LSD so they'd peak as the show began.

They waited for the last bell to ring and swallowed the tabs in the high school bathroom. Then, stepping casually from the building, Eddie and Clint walked a few blocks to join the students and parents gathered to watch the grade school's Halloween parade.

Little kids circled around the grass playground in their costumes. Several children had dressed as ghosts, the simple outfits surprisingly realistic as their sheets trailed on the lawn behind them.

"Check out the frog," Eddie commented. A child in the parade kept stumbling. He or she wore a gauze frog head mask, buttoned onto a green and yellow frog suit. The child wore snorkeling flippers on its hands and feet, and every few steps the flippers fell off.

"Hey, there's the Wicked Witch of the West." Her green papier-mâché mask had a pointy nose with black pins as hairs stuck into the end.

Clint and Eddie admired the costumes for a few more minutes. "Do you feel different?" Clint asked.

"Not yet."

"Me neither. Maybe it won't be much of anything after all."

The drug still hadn't kicked in when they headed into the woods that bordered the school. They trudged along a dirt path, packed hard by the feet of truant students. Sunshine dappled the trees as birds twittered. When they left the woods and stepped out into the street, the swoosh of cars surprised them. Both felt an unfamiliar, edgy buzz begin. They crossed the road and lingered, talking on the sidewalk. It was already four in the afternoon.

Eddie looked at Clint. "What are we planning to do again?"

"*The Wizard of Oz!*" Clint finally recalled.

"I should take my equipment home first. I'll meet you at your place," Eddie said, and headed home. He went in through the back door and closed it quietly. The doorway frame began bulging ever so gently in and out. Wood grain flowed like water as he watched. Eddie dropped the bag with his sports gear. He stared, fascinated, as the wood dissolved and reformed in wavy patterns.

Kyle was already home. "What're you staring at?" His brother came over and examined the door; he frowned and looked more closely at Eddie. "God, your pupils are dilated!" Kyle placed thumb and forefinger together at his lips and mimicked inhaling. "Strong dope?"

Eddie placed his palms together and mimed the beating of a birds' wings, flying off to Never-Never Land. "Clint and I dropped that acid I told you about."

Kyle moved closer and pointed to the stairs. "Watch out," he suggested, and lowered his voice. "Bad news. Mom's home from work."

"And?"

"And she's on her seasonal clean house mission."

"Crap! Thanks for the heads-up. I think I'm starting to trip for real."

"Those three little initials, L, S, and D? They'll get you every time." His red-headed brother grimaced. "My one time was *more* than enough. It felt like this." Kyle made his tall body go slack and he stroked the doorjamb with an expression of vacant wonder.

There was a thud on the ceiling and a machine started. A vacuum cleaner began bumping around furniture in the upstairs bedrooms. It swooshed *louder*, then softer, *louder*, then softer as it progressed across the floor.

Eddie's attention was drawn by the oversized framed photographs hanging in the hallway. In one of them he and Kyle were little boys: they stood in the middle of a greenhouse covered by dozens of butterflies. Their father had taken the photograph a decade earlier and captured the wonder of a moment of childhood, his children stock still in amazement at the ephemeral creatures that had alit on them. Now, while Eddie scrutinized them, the butterflies in the photo began flying. They rose from the boys in the photo. Butterflies fluttered in circles around their heads and left moving trails of glittery sparks in rainbow colors in the air behind them.

Belatedly Eddie realized his brother was asking him a question.

"This is your first acid trip, right?" Kyle repeated.

"Yeah." Eddie spun in a circle, staring round the hallway.

"There you are!" The brothers moved away from the photograph as their mother called from the landing at the top of the stairs. "Your sister already started vacuuming. I could use your help in the living room. This house is a mess!"

"On my way, Mom," Kyle called up the stairs.

"That'd be great, Kyle." She looked over the banister and exclaimed when she spotted Eddie. "You're home too? Good!"

"Uh, I'm watching *The Wizard of Oz* at Clint's," Eddie began.

"What time?" Mrs. Cooper was in painter's overalls, dressed for her battle with home entropy. She was armed with a bucket filled with cleaning products and rags and looked frighteningly efficient.

"It starts at seven."

"Then you've got plenty of time to help me out first." Her voice was crisp. "You do know this is not a request, right?"

"It's Halloween!"

"All the more reason to get it done and over with. I think once a year everyone can help out."

"Whatever you say, Mom, no prob." The boys began climbing the stairs.

"Ed," she continued, "grand prize. You get to clean out the refrigerator. I seriously doubt it's been cleaned since summer, and here it is almost November already. Besides, you're the one who's been asking, *what died in the fridge?* for weeks now."

Eddie stumbled.

Kyle clapped a hand on his brother's shoulder. "Eddie, you idiot, why'd you come home? You should've stayed outside," Kyle murmured. Placing his lips next to Eddie's right ear he suggested, "Steady on, dude. If you wear gloves you shouldn't catch anything. I think." Kyle bounded up the last top steps, to give his brother time to recover. In a loud voice he asked, "Mom, what do you want done first?"

She began to run through the mental lists she carried in her head. "Well," she said, "for starters, the recycling. Start with all the piles of newspapers and magazines."

"You sure you don't want to keep any of them? Even the cooking magazines? Any old articles or recipes?" Kyle purposely distracted her, and Eddie made it to the kitchen alone.

He stood in the center of the room and faced the tall family refrigerator. It was avocado green, the color of bile. When did they collect so many refrigerator magnets? The doors and one of the sides were covered with magnets from museums, national parks, and tacky tourist spots. Why look, there was one from Coney Island, its Ferris wheel magically whirling….

"Ed! Don't just stand there! That refrigerator's not going to clean itself!" His mother threw the comment at him from the doorway and returned to the living room.

Eddie looked at the kitchen clock, tocking noisily. He had stared at the multitude of magnets for over twenty minutes.

He opened the refrigerator and forced himself to really look at its crowded shelves. There were far too many opened bottles: expired juices, sodas gone flat, soured milk. Eddie transferred every liquid past its consumption date to the sink and dumped them out. Clots of milk plopped out, and fluids in strange colors swirled. As the last liquid glug glug glugged down the drain, he could *swear* he heard a burp.

Next, Eddie pulled out a vegetable bin and set it on the counter. He rubbed his face hard when he saw its contents. *Steady, now.* He retrieved the garbage can from under the sink and found a package of unused household cleaning gloves in a drawer. Kyle had spoken truly: the task called for rubber gloves. Actually, this job called for surgical quality, operating room protection.

Gloves on, he sorted through kind-of still-edible food; a family of five, especially one with three teenagers all engaged in high school sports, goes through a lot of groceries. He could salvage the root vegetables and onions that were only a little soft. He uncovered the leaves of brown lettuce, limp carrot sticks and wilted fronds of celery, and they began waving to him for help. Thanks to the chemicals washing through his brain, a bag of old potatoes sent out tendrils as he watched. *Purple*, Eddie registered from a place far, far away. He dropped the mushy vegetables in the garbage.

He uncovered wrinkled grapes, desiccated peaches, and a mushy melon half covered in saran wrap. *Go ahead, touch us*, they dared. He reached for the fruit. They dissolved, gooey, and his stomach lurched. Was this really happening, or was it the effects of the hit of acid? Was this trip going to turn into a bummer? Maybe he could still change places with Kyle.

His mother's voice came from the living room. "Just take down all those tchotchkes and set them on the coffee table," she directed.

The living room was crammed with mementos. Sports trophies and framed family photographs crowded most of the shelves; the rest held his parents' collection of southwest pottery. Eddie couldn't go anywhere near the living room. He would drop every breakable to smash on the floor. He stood at the kitchen sink and swayed, trying hard to think. Something clammy brushed his arm where the glove ended. He had made contact with a composting zucchini that was spotted with mold.

The slime that came off began crawling on his skin.

"Euaaah!" Eddie grabbed a sponge and scrubbed his skin; the fluorescent specks faded and finally vanished.

"Ed?" his mom called. "Ed? Everything okay in there?"

"It's all good!" His words sounded as if they were emerging from the far end of a tube.

*Focus*. He pulled out the second bin. It contained a bunch

of mottled bananas, all somehow still attached to a writhing stalk. Eddie swallowed hard and tipped the bin's contents into the trash. *Jars*, he thought. *Jars. Anything is better than this.*

Slowly, carefully, using both hands, one by one he removed the Mason jars crowding the two bottom refrigerator shelves. His face reflected, elongated and distorted, off a glass of pickling spices. *Poppies,* a voice cackled in an evil whisper.

The first Mason jar he opened held homemade pickles. A dill sprig pirouetted and curtsied for him. *Nice*, Eddie thought, and began to relax. But the next three jars were science projects gone bad. Olives in a cloudy clump. Mayonnaise – about a thousand years ago. A jam jar next. Strawberry jam morphed into a mold factory topped by a layer of lime green fur before his eyes. He threw the jars in the garbage.

Nervous, Eddie opened a container of chunky peanut butter. *No problem. Phew. Hey – I can't smell a thing*! Eddie realized that the hit of LSD had probably affected his sense of smell. Bad enough imagining the stink of all the rotting food. He smiled, grateful, as his brain went on playing tricks.

The smile vanished when he spotted the large Tupperware bowl at the back of the last shelf of the refrigerator. Eddie held his breath and cracked the lid. Little fuzzy life forms began creeping up the sides, whispering to each other. They multiplied, swelling with oxygen as the air swooshed in. They came, they crept faster and faster and faster and…. He shoved the lid back on and held the container out at arm's length to hurl into the garbage. *Breathe in, breathe out*, Eddie prayed silently. *I am high as hell and tripping my brains out.*

The fabric of the present shredded. The boundary between the real and the imaginary was a flimsy barrier. Eddie discovered that its edges were porous: when he reached out his hand, the kitchen sink shimmered and floated towards his reach.

"So, Ed!"

He jumped at the sound of his mother's voice.

She stood at the door to the kitchen, her arms filled with a huge stack of magazines. "Did you find what died in there?"

"Only half the fridge, Mom."

She ignored the sarcasm as her eyes took in the heaps of dead vegetables and hazard of bottles and jars in the garbage. She frowned. "Are you throwing out my Tupperware containers? *Empty* them and put them in the dishwasher. Hey! The homemade strawberry jam!" she exclaimed. "We just opened that jar!"

Eddie was incapable of answering her. He couldn't respond, because his hold on the material world – on any reality - was slipping away. He looked away fast before she could notice his dilated eyes.

*My dilated I's*, he thought.

His mind wandered off, following a LSD flight out of linguistic reality. His mother went on talking, but her words made no sense. Dimensions were collapsing. The walls and ceiling absorbed language. His mother spoke, but the pulsing room snatched the words away before they reached Eddie.

*Why can't I track this conversation?* he groaned.

All at once he could hear her again. Her voice echoed, and he both heard and saw the trails of her words chasing themselves around the room. "Well, set them in the sink and someone can take care of those later," she said absently. She shifted the lopsided stack in her arms and walked over to examine the garbage more closely. "Did you throw out perfectly good vegetables?"

"Hey Ed," Kyle called out. "Didn't you say you're watching *The Wizard of Oz* at Clint's?"

"Right!" *The Wizard of Oz!* He'd forgotten all about it. He risked a glance at the clock and was shocked to realize hours had passed since he began the challenge of cleaning the refrigerator. "It starts in a few minutes." Eddie kept his face tilted away from his mother.

She went on inspecting his progress. "Come on, Ed! A lot of these jars can be rinsed out and just put in the dishwasher. You know I reuse all of my canning stuff."

In his addled brain he told her, "Mom, no way I'm going anywhere back near the garbage. The bin is glowing, don't you see? *The Invasion of the Body Snatchers* is in there. And they are lurking, they are. They're waiting for me." With telepathy he warned her, not needing to speak the words aloud. Why didn't she hear him?

"Mom, you've got to be kidding." Kyle hurried into the kitchen. He took her elbow, positioning himself so that his tall body blocked her view of Eddie. "Ed did us all a favor. Did *you* want to face what's left in some of those jars?"

She wrinkled her nose. "Probably not," she admitted. "Although…." Her voice trailed off. "You know what? Do me a favor? Scrub the inside with baking soda later? That should take care of any odors in the fridge itself. *Something sure stinks. Something's really, really acidic.*"

Eddie snorted, trying not to laugh. He caught Kyle's eye, and both burst into whoops of laughter. No matter how hard he tried once he began laughing Eddie could not stop. He bent over double, the tears in his eyes reflecting rainbows.

"What'd I say?" their mother asked.

Every time they opened their mouths they gasped and began laughing again.

"Very funny! Go ahead, laugh at your poor old mom. You kids! But you know," she mused, "I think I can use the leftovers from last night to pull a meal together. What about it? Kyle? Ed?"

Kyle looked over her shoulder and jerked his head in the direction of the front door.

Eddie edged around her, moving fast. "Um, I think I'll eat

supper at Clint's," he said, and began to run.

## THE RED WALLET

The rack by the door in the waiting room was heavy with damp raincoats. A circle of red and green, gold and silver shopping bags hid the floor around it.

"Bernice Fallon?"

A middle-aged woman, sitting on a chair in the corner, rose stiffly to her feet.

"Doctor Burnside will see you in a few minutes. If you'll just follow me...."

Bernice Fallon trailed a nurse to the adjoining room. Two hours later, she was the last patient to leave the medical office. Bernice shrugged into her coat and swept the remaining shopping bags up in her arms.

Doctor Burnside waved her to the door.

Bernice turned back, blocking the closing door with her foot.

The doctor's smile was practiced, professional. "Like we discussed, Bernice, all of these last tests are negative. Really. Take my advice." He hesitated as if he wanted to add something more but had changed his mind, saying only, "And, have a good Christmas."

"You, too." Disappointed, Bernice had to turn her head away. Even to her ears the words sounded reluctant.

She held her shopping bags firmly as she pushed the elevator button. Bernice relived the consultation as the elevator descended.

"Another negative test result," she commented in a flat tone. For three months, she had insisted on tests. For three months, the good doctor had insisted that Bernice was ridiculously healthy. "Seven different exams, and not one of them can find what's wrong with me. Why?"

"Because you don't have cancer, and you don't have the coronavirus. There are no grounds for concern for either sickness. You don't have anything else, either," he'd told her. "I'm going to give you something for the cough and your palpitations." He held up a palm before he wrote out the prescriptions. "For your anxiety, not for a heart condition. Bernice, relax. After the holidays I will refer you, if you still want that. But believe me, you aren't sick."

"If I'm not sick, then who is?"

Doctor Burnside hadn't given her an answer then, and neither did the empty elevator now. Bernice turned around, restless and sullen, staring at the back wall.

When she finally registered the fact that a red wallet lay on the floor, Bernice groaned. It probably belonged to another patient. No way she wanted to head back to the office and face her doctor again.

The elevator reached the ground floor and the doors slid open. Bernice peered out into the lobby. She didn't see any of the security guards; only the unblinking security cameras watched. She picked up the wallet and tossed it in one of her bags.

When she arrived home, she dropped her purchases on the kitchen table and turned on the stove burner below the tea kettle. She checked her cell phone and saw her mother had called. Bernice didn't call back, knowing how the conversation would go.

"Stop being a hypochondriac!" her mother repeatedly told her. Every time she called her mother insisted, "Trust me, Bernice. No one should know the date they can expect to meet death."

She seated herself as the blue flames flickered. "Well." Bernice went on talking to herself. "I've got a free evening and won't be dying anytime soon. Might as well go through what I bought. I can wrap presents and assign tags, and that'll be over for another twelve months."

Bernice reached into the first bag and pulled out the hard edges of oversized coffee table books. Glossy recipes of the foods of Asia, bridges spanning the U.S.A.'s rivers and lakes, Coco Channel's best creations. When in doubt, a nice coffee table book was the ideal gift. "One size fits all," she muttered. *Janet, Roy, Stephen.* She wrote the names one under another in a column. "All three probably like art books, and God knows Stephen's a fashionista. Fashionisto?"

She stacked the books on her left and from the bag she next pulled out a silk scarf. Eighty dollars! She had paid way more than she planned, selecting it from the top of a pile on the front counter at Macy's without checking the price. "Hm. I can keep this for myself."

Bernice turned her attention to a new umbrella, and for the first time that day she was happy. The afternoon rainstorm had reminded her that her aide always lost his umbrellas; each year she provided him with a replacement. *Geoffrey, umbrella,* she wrote, and opened the next bag.

"What in the world? Oh! The wallet I found in the elevator." Frowning, Bernice turned the fat, deluxe size porte-monnaie in her hands. The red leather was soft, clearly a well-used personal item. "Who do I give you back to?"

Bernice unsnapped the clasp and felt strangely illicit as she did so, like a trespasser. Fifty-three bucks' cash, receipts for as yet unclaimed post office packages, credit cards. She pulled out a VISA card that bore the name Cecily Blake, valid until January, about to expire.

The lights in her kitchen reflected off an employee ID hologram. Cecily Blake, African American, head slightly tilted. Cecily looked like she was about forty years old. Bernice examined membership cards for The Nature Conservancy, Congressional Caucus on Black Women and Girls, and a family card for the metropolitan library. Those memberships were expiring, too.

She slipped her fingers into a pocket and extracted photos sheathed in a protective plastic envelope. Cecily stood on a deserted beach, surrounded by stacks of plastic bins with big labels. Bernice identified Specimen Batch #33 and Specimen Batch #34. Cecily wore jeans and boots covered with sand and a pleased smile.

Four children looked out from the next photo. They ranged from a toddler to a teenaged boy with braces; Cecily and a bald man stood behind them. Xmas 2019, someone had written on the back of the photograph. "Your husband and family," Bernice spoke to the photograph. "Cool. The kids all look like you!"

In the third photo Cecily wore a solemn expression and a dark robe with a golden yellow hood. "Smart. Doctoral degree, along with being wife, mom, and researcher," Bernice murmured. "You go, girl." She held out the picture to see it better. Cecily looked tired. Her cheeks looked too thin.

Bernice placed the personal photos and credit cards on top of the pile of coffee table books. She had identified the owner of the wallet but couldn't bring herself to stop exploring its contents. "Yeah, yeah, I'm snooping. Let's pretend; let's say, I'm a detective."

A zippered pocket held folded sheets of paper and some index cards. Bernice read the first one. Cecily had made notations in varying colors of ink. *Dion – microphone + 6 more months' voice lessons. Terri – gift certificate for pierced ears and earrings to be used day she turns 16. Kofi – B&B weekend, memories album.*

A note on the other side of the card read: *Organic basket for Ronette.* Whoever Ronette was, Cecily knew she preferred natural foods. *Theater tickets and goodbye notes for Jonathan, Lisa and Clarice.*

Bernice shivered. It felt like someone just walked on top of her grave. "Why are these names familiar?" Then she realized: all three worked in Doctor Burnside's office. "Cecily, aren't you returning after the holidays? Why such lavish gifts?

And, why the goodbye notes?"

*Wendie* was the next name on the list, but the notes in blue didn't continue.

Bernice unfolded a badly wrinkled sheet of paper. "No. No. Oh my God. Oh, shit." Bernice's face paled. Her voice died away as she read through the medical terminology she somehow still, fatalistically, expected to receive. "Metastases, white cell count, blood work results. Stage four." Cecily had crumpled those words, then smoothed them back out and folded the sad news in two.

She'd begun a list on the back side, this one in purple ink.

Bernice stopped reading Cecily's notes out loud. Quiet now, she sat in her warm kitchen and made herself read and reread the remaining notes. *Living will. Hospice, arrangements for home death. Assisted? Video (DO THIS FIRST): "Baby girl, you're only twenty months old but know that Momma loves you, now and forever. I'm with the Lord and the angels now. And I am always by you, your own private angel."* The words were hard to make out, blurry and splotched. Bernice imagined Cecily's tears falling as she wrote the love note to the young daughter who would barely remember her.

Bernice reluctantly turned to the final item from the wallet. It was not a photo or a note. The last piece was a donor's card, signed December 4. A week ago. *Corneas only,* Cecily's signature in ink as red as blood.

Bernice replaced everything back in the wallet and set it exactly in front of her on the table. She jumped when the kettle on the stove whistled. "Hot water," she thought. "And suddenly I am so glad I'm not in it." She turned off the stove, poured boiling water over a tea bag, and went on staring at the red wallet.

Bernice and her tea steeped. When had her bitterness and fear begun? How much time had she lost, inventing maladies to avoid embracing being alive?

What would it be like, knowing you really were about to

die, planning for the event? She heard her mother's voice, insisting that no one should know the date they would die.

Bernice lifted her mug and sipped tea without tasting it as she reached for her cell phone.

When the medical office's answering service spoke, Bernice cleared her throat. "Hello, this is Bernice Fallon, I'm a patient of Doctor Burnside and I need to leave him a message. I have something belonging to one of his other patients. I found Cecily Blake's wallet this afternoon as I was leaving the building. I'll bring it by on Monday. But I need to cancel all my remaining appointments.... Tell Doctor Burnside, I'm taking his advice to try and relax more. Thank you, Merry Christmas to you, too. What's that? Do I have plans for New Year's? Strangely enough, I think I do. I need to make some New Year's resolutions. And last-minute travel reservations, no, no idea yet where.

"But I think I want to go to the beach."

## PRINCESS RAIN CLOUDS

"This one?" Laura lifted the arm hanging out the car window to point a finger at the lake. "Is this one it?" The vacation towns repeated themselves: a small downtown that consisted of one or two blocks, a placid body of water ringed with trees, and a necklace of wooden cabins strung along the shoreline. Each lake was attractive, and all of them looked the way she imagined Crystal Lake must.

Ethan Schroyer shook his head and grinned over at his girlfriend. "Wrong again."

"I'm tired of guessing. Remind me, which relatives am I meeting?"

"All of them. My parents. My brothers and sister." Ethan ticked off a list of names. "Dawn is nine, Dominick seven, Ryan thirteen. My other relatives are driving out today. My dad's brother Don and his wife, Lena. Their older son works in Wyoming, but they have a new boy, Ricky. All of my cousins are oopsie babies." Ethan added, "Gifts from God. Including the Podolski kids."

"The kids we were supposed to bring?"

"Yeah. You'll like them."

"How about Hannah?"

He laughed with pleasure. "*Especially* Princess Rain Clouds."

"But her real name's Hannah, right?"

"We call her Princess Rain Clouds because she's so gloomy. I was going to pick up Princess and Jake, her brother. Uncle Fred had some excuse for why he couldn't come. Then he decided he could come after all. I always feel sorry for Hannah. My aunt and uncle are poster children for bad parenting." Ethan drove on for another ten minutes and finally left the main road. "Here's our turn off."

"This little road?"

The trees to their left darkened into forest as sunlight on the water glittered, Crystal Lake winking as they passed camps. There were lots of boats on the lake and only Ethan's car on the gravel road. Gravel crunching under the tires, Ethan pulled in next to his parents' station wagon and parked.

A large dog (part sheep dog, part pointer, part blue heeler) barked as it raced across the property. "Bello!" Ethan called out, and Bello's tail beat a frenetic tattoo against the car door. The dog whined with joy.

"Come on, babe. Let's go meet my family." Ethan got out of the car. "C'mere, you mutt!"

Bello jump on him, ecstatic.

"Hang on," Laura said. "I'm not ready. I think I'm nervous."

Ethan reached in the window and patted her head. "Bello here will just lick you to death. He loves on everything except other dogs."

"Maybe it's not the dog I'm worried about."

Ethan laughed at her. "It's okay. You're safe. My brother Ryan's barely housebroken, but no one bites."

She stayed in the car, looking out the open window at the lake. Laura heard the slap of badly wielded boat oars and the quacks of flying ducks. Woods filled the shoreline all around the cabin and the closest home was far away, just visible through the trees. The Schroyer family cabin was painted green and brown to blend in with the forest. A picnic table jutted out beyond the north side. A clothesline sagged with laundry and a dripping life jacket.

The more she concentrated, the clearer she could hear waves whoosh as they hit the shore. Laura and Ethan had completed their first year at college, and Laura hadn't considered just how remote the cabin was. She sighed, then began to laugh. "You could have warned me. Being at Crystal Lake is nothing like being in the city, is it?" she called out the window to Ethan.

He wrestled with the happy dog as he waited for her. "Embrace the boredom. You'll love it."

"I can't wait to meet Princess Rain Clouds," she said, and opened the car door.

☐

Hannah Podolski was overjoyed when they left for Crystal Lake. Her dad had suddenly changed his mind and agreed to spend the holiday weekend with her mother's brothers and their families. Five of Hannah's Schroyer cousins would be there. Princess Rain Clouds, they called her. Her cousin Ethan had christened her with the nickname, and it had stuck. Hannah didn't mind. They called her Princess! She was amazed that they cared enough to give her a nickname at all.

Three tense hours after leaving home, her brother parked at the cabin and climbed out. Fred got out of the passenger side, looking shaky; he had let Jake drive.

Her parents were still arguing as Fred held the door for her mother. "Tammy, I'm here, aren't I? What do you want from me? I asked a hundred times, let's fly to Vegas, just the two of us. See a few shows, no kids along. But no-o-o: it had to be Crystal Lake."

No one spoke, and Hannah heard off-key singing coming from the shoreline.

Her father winced. "The Schroyers, tone-deaf about music, about life, about private relationships. Drown me Lord," he muttered, "drown me now. Come on, Hannah. Let's go!"

Her legs stuck to the car vinyl. On long car rides the elastic band of her shorts dug into her body, and she had welts on her tummy and the middle of her thighs. Hannah climbed clumsily out of the back seat. Her hair was an in-between length of the shade known in grown women as dishwater blonde.

In defiance of excellent genes, Hannah was uncomfortable in her skin. Her bones still carried baby fat on them, and she refused to let her mother lead her over to the clothes racks with larger sizes at the discount store out at the mall. "Those are for big girls," she insisted.

The Schroyers came running up from the lake to greet them. Ryan and Dominick had freckles and everyone except Ethan was already tanned. Hannah saw that Ethan had a girl with him, and that she was pretty.

Ryan whistled shrilly through the gap in his front teeth. "It's the puddle skiing cousins!" he shrieked.

Hannah did not know how Dawn survived the misfortune of three brothers. Having one brother was bad enough. "You know it's Podolski," she said. "And your nickname's just, Squirt! Besides, who ever heard of skiing puddles?"

"Who peed in *your* corn flakes this morning?" he retorted.

"Princess," Dom added, "did you forget to take your nice pill?"

Uncle Aaron lifted Hannah for a hug. "Quiet down there, everyone. Princess Rain Clouds, it's only your silly Schroyer cousins talking." Uncle Aaron hugged his sister Tammy next and acknowledged his brother-in-law with a muted "Hey, Fred."

☐

Hannah and her brother clustered with their cousins in the cabin's screened-in porch. "What'd you catch this summer?" she asked.

Dom was carefully lifting a cardboard box out of a wide mesh wire cage. "A flying squirrel! We named him Rocky. Right now, he's sleeping. Flying squirrels are nocturnal. That means they wake and get active at night." Dom pointed at the wall. "Rocky likes to fly around the porch. We helped Dad build a home for him!"

Hannah saw that Uncle Aaron, with the help of the children, had erected platforms around the backside of the fireplace.

"And he really flies?"

"No, Princess," Dawn answered. "Rocky has webs of skin between his legs and torso. They spread when he leaps to give him flight conductivity." Like all the Schroyers, Dawn's speech became pedantic when she got the chance to explain something. But Hannah wasn't listening. Exclaiming, she crowded close as Dom gently lifted a tiny furry body out of the box and handed the creature to Ryan. Large black eyes looked at her.

"He kind of looks like a chipmunk. Can I hold him next?" Hannah put out a hand.

Ryan shook his head. "Mom says, never disturb him during the daytime. But we wanted to show you him. Tonight when he's active we'll let him out of the cage for a while. When Rocky gets used to you, he'll eat out of your hands!"

"What else have you got?"

"Alive or dead?"

Hannah looked at Dom in horror.

"She means animals that are living, as in, breathing," Jake prompted.

"You remember the ranger camp on the north end of the lake?" Dom asked. "Dad knows the head ranger. He brought us Rocky. Remember how last year they brought us a flicker with a broken wing?"

"So, this year we have Rocky, one diamond back turtle,

and three frogs," Dawn listed proudly. "We had a garter snake, but Mom made me let it go already. We put all the others in the fish cage out by the dock for the summer; we'll let them go later. We have to keep Bello away from the frogs, though! That dumb dog thinks he can eat them!"

"The turtles and frogs we catch ourselves," said Dom.

"I caught the frogs!" Ryan broke in.

"Sure, you did, Squirt," amended Dom. "But I caught the turtle."

"Only because it was too slow to get away from you!"

"The dead critters are a bug collection I started," Dom continued.

"Like I just said, the dead can't run away."

"We'll let the living critters go on our last day at the lake," Dawn corrected Dom.

"Dom, how do you stand being interrupted all the time?" Jake asked.

Hannah knew why: her cousins weren't competitive with one another. They just liked to be sure visitors got the facts straight. She listened, tasting a familiar sour jealousy. Her father was allergic to cats. And dogs. And anything with feathers. They had talked Fred into a tank of guppies one Christmas, and before Easter the fish had floated belly up, covered in lurid, fuzzy moss. That was her family's single venture into pet ownership.

She made a face, just like the one her father had made in the car when they first arrived. "Frogs, yuck. They're slippery."

"They're amphibians," Dawn informed her. "They're not slippery, they have to keep their skins moist. Let's swim out to the dock and look at them!"

"Then we'll be all wet."

Dawn put an arm around her cousin. "Come on Princess, it'll be fun. When you're wet, if you pick one up you won't even notice how slippery they are." Dawn insisted that

Hannah come with them.

Complaining happily, Hannah changed into her bathing suit and trailed her cousins and Laura down to the water. She was less brittle with the special present her cousins gave her: the gift of their attention. But she paused at the edge of the lake, suddenly cowed. Laura wore a bikini and in Hannah's eight-year-old eyes she was beautiful in a way impossible to imagine for herself. Even Dawn was taller than Hannah, and self-assured amid a family of boys. She would never be like Laura or Dawn. Why was she born so awkward?

Ethan watched Hannah shivering at the water's edge. "I'll give you a ride," he offered, seeing but not understanding her fear. "You don't have to worry about anyone dunking you." Ethan lifted her onto his shoulders and waded out in the water.

Hannah shrieked with joy. She waited for the day when her favorite cousin would refrain from boosting her onto his shoulders and Dawn would stop asking her to come along. If she was with her cousins, she was safe.

□

Uncle Don and Aunt Lena arrived thirty minutes later. Their older son had moved cross country, and their toddler Ricky slept with his mouth open and his head on one side in his car seat in the back of the SUV. Red-haired and cherubic, Ricky was the youngest cousin.

The kids were out on the dock, so only Aaron and Jeri walked out to greet them. They hugged the new arrivals with real warmth.

"Fred's here," Aaron relayed. "Tammy talked him into coming."

"Gracing us with his presence." Don lifted Ricky out of his car seat and handed him to Lena. "And a fun time will be had by all."

"Don, every family has its moments.... But I have to say, Fred and Tammy sure are tense. Things at home must be pretty bad," said Jeri.

"The last time I saw her Tammy said she's been getting weird looks in town, and people are still talking. An eleven-car pileup in the fog! She says, Fred's still really shook up. Everyone thinks he caused the accident. And, guess what. You know what I was told? Fred had a female passenger with him in the truck."

"And you believe the rumors?" asked Lena as she handed her brother-in-law a suitcase.

"Lena, we all know Fred. What do you think?"

"Where *are* Fred and Tammy?"

"At the picnic table. Fred's enjoying how nicely Ethan's girlfriend Laura fills out her bikini," Aaron said. "He's practically drool - "

"Well, hello Princess!" Lena interrupted loudly.

The adults turned: Hannah, wet in her dripping bathing suit, had just come out of the cabin.

"I needed to go to the bathroom," she apologized, and ran back to the lake before anyone could say anything.

"Oh God, that poor child." Lena kissed the top of her sleeping son's head. "Let's see if we can make it through just one visit without a fight."

☐

Late that afternoon, before the sun sank, the fathers and kids erected tents. Jake and his father tamped tent stakes into the root beds of thick grass while Hannah watched. Fred's handsome face was red and the skin around his eyes was tight. He flexed his fingers. He disliked using his hands for anything but driving, and even then he always wore driving gloves.

Fred wrestled with the tent in frustration.

"Need some help there, Fred?"

"Christ, Aaron, don't you ever mow this place?"

"Nope. It's lakefront property to a cabin in the woods, Fred, not a lawn in the suburbs," Aaron answered mildly. He was preoccupied with the Weber grill, prepping it for the meats to come. And he pushed rocks into place for the fire pit, making their circle bigger. "Somewhere you'd rather be?"

"Honestly? I swear to God, Aaron, if I wanted to erect a tent, I would have moved to Maine and bought stock in goddamn L.L. Bean."

"Hey!" exclaimed Jake. "Dad! Did you get a new tattoo?"

"I want to see it too!" Hannah moved closer and her father rolled up his shirtsleeve to show them the red Celtic knot on his right forearm.

Uncle Don scrutinized it. "Nice," he commented. "But, a Celtic design? Sure and begorrah, it's the Clan Podolski out of Ireland's Glenballyemon."

Hannah giggled. "You talk funny, Uncle Don!"

Aaron glanced sidelong at the tattoo but only asked, "Hey Jake, you got any experience building fires?"

"Does building them on the beach qualify?"

"It does. Okay, you're on. Tonight, you light the fire pit."

"What's the point of a fancy grill when you've got a fire pit?" Fred asked off-handedly. "Really, I'd like to know."

"S'mores. Marshmallows. Hot dogs on sticks. I don't know, a bed of coals to gaze into in the dark." Aaron turned his back and went back to tending his grill.

□

Hannah sat, absorbed, listening as Aunt Lena and her mom talked and joked with Aunt Jeri. Jeri was stirring a huge pot of spaghetti sauce, and the kitchen smelled of garlic, tomatoes, onions, and peppers. Hannah jumped when Ryan and Dom banged noisily into the room. Their siblings were already waiting to be assigned tasks.

"Right on time," Jeri said when she saw the boys. "Okay kids. Ethan, dishes to the table. Dominick, silverware for everyone. Ryan, milk pitcher on the kids' table. Sodas in the cooler. Ryan, do *not* pour anything! Let people pick for themselves what they want to drink." Aunt Jeri paused and thought. "Dawn, give everyone a napkin. Better yet, put a pile of napkins in the middle of both tables. Salt and pepper shakers. Salad dressings and the grated cheese, too. Extra barbeque sauce. Don't try to carry everything at once! You can make two trips, you know! Come back for the rest."

Hannah looked on as Aunt Jeri directed her children. They were as efficient as a staff at a café – if zombies had staffed that café.

"Yes, mistress," intoned Ryan. "I'm programmed to obey. Must not drop sodas. Must not drop sodas." He promptly dropped an armful of cans.

"Correction to program," he droned. "Correction to program, must not *spill* sodas."

Ryan collected the cans as his mother tried hard not to laugh. "And that, kiddo, is why you don't get to pour drinks for anyone anymore."

"Mom, if he perches my glass of milk on the edge of the table today, I swear I'll make you and Dad put him up for adoption!" Dawn threatened.

Tammy spoke up. "Hannah, you can help Dawn."

"No! Hang on there, Princess."

Hannah froze, waiting for her mother and her aunt to tell her what to do. Aunt Jeri explained, "I've said it before: all my kids have to help out. I'm not going to make Dawn a servant to a house full of brothers."

"Early training for the boys," contributed Aunt Lena.

"That's right," said Aunt Jeri. "It's a brave new world, and I want my sons to appreciate the women they marry."

"Before they turn them into servants," Tammy finished.

All three women glanced at Hannah.

Aunt Jeri gave her a pitying smile. "The water isn't quite boiling yet. When it does, Princess Rain Clouds, how about you hand me the spaghetti?" she requested as she turned back to the stove.

☐

The barbequed chicken was crispy, the hotdogs and burgers grilled, the pasta cooked, and everyone seated. The kids sat at the picnic table, and the adults used the folding table Ethan and his father carried off the screened porch and onto the grass.

Hannah frowned at the plate her mother handed to her: it held a hamburger patty and an oversized portion of salad. She sat across from Ryan, who grinned evilly.

"Would you like a soda, jerk?"

Hannah leaned to the side, but she wasn't fast enough. Ryan squirted a mouthful of soda all over the front of her shirt.

Ryan could squirt fluids with an amazing range through the gap in his teeth. "Ha ha ha! I've been practicing! Eating outdoors: no muss, no fuss. I love being at the cabin. Learn to love it or learn to duck!"

"Zzz zer Zzz zer." Dawn pulled an imaginary string back and forth from her ears. "Squirt began leaking brains at birth. He's been pulling this stunt ever since." Ryan squirted juice at his sister, but she ducked fast.

"Knock knock?"

"Who's there?"

"Dawn."

"Dawn who?"

"Dawn of the Dead! That's hilarious!" Ryan gleefully banged his hands on the table and hit his plate. His food somersaulted in the air and landed on the grass.

Bello dashed over before Ryan could react and began wolfing down meatballs. Hannah and her cousins shrieked with laughter.

"This is why all our dishes here at the cabin are plastic, Princess," said Dawn. "This is why Ryan gets banned for life from restaurants."

◻

The Schroyer camp insisted on a 'No going in the water until thirty minutes after eating' rule. Most of the kids waited impatiently until they could return to the dock. Hannah didn't go swimming again when she saw Ethan and Laura had stayed behind. Also, she didn't want to squirm back into her damp bathing suit.

The constellation of bodies shifted as the adults moved over to the redwood table. They lit cigarettes and replenished plates and drinks or opened new beers. Fred casually moved to sit across from Laura. Hannah's aunts and uncles discussed the possibility of Jake going to work for Aaron.

"Aaron, he's a responsible kid," her mother said.

"Jake would do a decent job," Uncle Don agreed.

"Nice to get your official stamp of approval for my children at least."

Uncle Don snorted. "No one's insulting you. Christ, Fred!"

The porch lights cast a yellow light into the lake; the flicker of globe candles set along the top of the picnic table lit up faces. Ethan murmured with his girlfriend. Her cousins were leaving the water now, trailing noisily back to the cabin; Hannah felt abandoned. None of Hannah's aunts and uncles or parents paid any attention to her.

*I might as well be invisible. Would anyone notice if all of a sudden, I wasn't here? Would anyone even miss me?* She hesitated, considering the darkening air around the picnic table. Then, as Princess Rain Clouds, she slipped off the bench, got down on all fours and ducked under the table.

"I'll talk with Jake this weekend," Uncle Aaron's voice assented from above the tabletop. She crawled further and planted her palm in the pile of spaghetti on the ground beneath the bench where Ryan had been sitting. Bello had eaten the meatballs and ignored most of the pasta.

Hannah wiped her hand on the grass and went on crawling towards Ethan. She was going to surprise him for sure! Hannah reached Ethan's feet, looked up, and froze.

Ethan's hand was on Laura's thigh, less than six inches from Hannah's face. His fingers crept in and out of the top of her cut-offs; Laura kept batting the fingers away with her left hand. Hannah didn't see Laura's other hand, because his shirttails were tugged out and hid the top of his jeans. Ethan entwined his leg around Laura's.

Hannah reared back and banged her head hard on the table.

Aunt Jeri's head appeared as hands fumbled their way back out from under the table. "Princess! What in the world are you doing?"

She looked at her aunt with no idea of how to answer the question.

"Come on out."

Hannah crept out from under the picnic bench as Laura surreptitiously tugged at her shorts. Laura's face had turned the mottled crimson of overripe strawberries.

Ethan kept his head lowered to avoid his mother's eyes.

"Princess, how about we go to the cabin; you can help me carry some of the empty plates." Aunt Jeri rose from the picnic table bench with a pointed look at her son.

Ethan smiled weakly. He placed his hands, fingers laced in Laura's, in prominent display on the top of the picnic table. "Look, Ma, no hands!"

"Manners, Ethan! Believe it or not, I was young once."

"Aunt Jeri, why are you trying not to laugh? What's so funny?" asked Hannah.

Uncle Aaron moved to take Hannah's place and Fred moved back to sit by Tammy. Aaron draped his arm over Ethan's shoulders. "I'm so glad you and Laura made it this weekend!" Uncle Aaron was getting a heat on, jocular and pleased with the world. "But what did you do to startle the Princess?"

☐

Up at the cabin Hannah found her cousins sorting sandals and sneakers out of the mound of footwear piled on the porch.

"We're going for a walk. Come with us!" Dom and Ryan begged.

"There's clean-up to be done," objected Aunt Jeri.

"Not everyone's finished eating," countered Dom.

"We are." Laura and Ethan had hastily left the picnic table and followed them to the cabin. "Your uncle keeps talking to me. He's way too friendly," Hannah heard her whisper to Ethan.

"You guys should come," Ryan insisted. "You too, Ethan! It will be fun and besides, Laura can carry one of the flashlights." Cannily, he included Ethan's girlfriend.

"Mom, we'll help you with clean-up later," Ethan offered.

Jeri sighed and gave in. "No we's about it. The moms will do the cleaning up."

This night, all the cousins took part in one last, common adventure. Laura took the second flashlight and the kids headed out the door. They fanned out on the road.

"Are you going to tell us where we're going?" Jake asked.

"Turn off the flashlights." Ryan halted and Hannah ran into his ankles in the dark. They walked on for five minutes before Ryan stopped again. "Now, listen up. Don't make any noise or we'll get caught. There's a religious retreat down the road. It doesn't matter which group rents it: they're all nutso. Dad gets mad if we make fun of them. He tells us, they aren't hurting anybody. And that a little more religion would be a good thing for the world. What does he know?" Ryan dismissed his parent's tolerance and faith with a wave of his hand.

"Dude!" Ethan and his brother high-fived. "Oh my God, I remember those lectures.... It's an interdenominational retreat, Laura," he explained. "Anyone can rent the space. We go spy on it once a year. This is the first time we've ever brought anyone else along to watch. I know exactly how mad Dad would be if he knew what we're doing." Ethan imitated Aaron's deep voice. "Kids, my idea of summer vacation includes concepts like *an escape from the rest of the world* and *privacy.*"

"Late at night they have real intense bonfire meetings," Ryan concluded. "If we're quiet, we can watch the whole thing!"

"That's not such a great idea," Hannah objected. It was one thing to feel invisible; it was another altogether to spy.

"You can't go back now," Dom said. "Dad will notice and want to know where we went. C'mon Princess Rain Clouds, don't be a spoilsport!"

"Who's a spoilsport!" Hannah defended herself hotly. "Good thing I'm not chicken, Dominick Schroyer."

They walked more slowly as their eyes adjusted to the summer night. She moved in front by Dom.

"You hear them?" he asked her.

Hannah made out the first sounds of singing and clapping hands.

"Everybody be quiet." Ryan ordered in a low voice. The road curved to the left, a short driveway branching steeply away. The cousins and Laura stood, straining their eyes in the dark to the tops of the hardwoods and pines that lined the gravel road. Stars glimmered high above behind a row of trees.

Dom whispered in Hannah's ear. "Over behind the hedges." The children, all of them trying not to breathe, crept along the thick, seven-foot high bushes. These had been planted for privacy and to keep the retreat attendants focused on the meetings. The architects may have considered the curiosity of neighbors, but not the peculiar, persistent ingenuity children possess.

Ryan still led. Holding hands, Ethan and Laura followed close behind, followed by Jake. Dom and Hannah were close on their heels and Dawn took the rear.

Hannah peered through the branches of the thick hedges. The buildings were arranged in a horseshoe shape, with a raised platform in the middle. A bonfire burned, sparks rising in the still night. The flames lit up colors in the gigantic, stained glass window of the big prayer and meditation center. Hannah could make out flickering figures in the panes: stars with points and a long-haired Christ. She also saw a snake, and the head of an elephant, and oversized hands.

Perhaps sixty people sat around the bonfire. Two women and a man holding guitars sat cross-legged on the raised platform. They resumed playing, nodding their heads as they began. "Oh, happy day," they sang.

Hannah was disappointed that the group of black, brown, and white Christians looked completely normal. People sat on blankets on the ground or in flimsy folding chairs set up on the grass. The worshippers wore summery short sleeves and sneakers or sandals; the scene was simply more casual than her own Catholic church on Sundays.

She watched the faces shining in the fire light.

"Oh, happy day!" A female voice, clear as a bell, suddenly rang out. The owner of the voice sat in the middle of a group on the grass. She was a heavyset girl, heavier than Hannah. It was hard to tell how big she was. Her long hair floated and she wore a dress that billowed out around her.

"Why is she wearing sunglasses?" Hannah asked, but none of her relatives answered. She stared at the ecstatic faces in the clearing. The voice of the girl sitting in the middle carried and rose. The group around the fire clapped their hands.

"Oh, happy day! Jesus walked on his way!" The voice of the girl on the lawn pealed with joy. She stood up, and for the first time Hannah saw the black dog laying patiently at the girl's feet. The girl raised her hands and her fingers fluttered to the verses. Other hands began to wave.

"Praise the Lord!" someone called. A big woman appeared from where she had been standing in the back. She had carrot-colored hair and a body shaped like a fat pear, and the tambourine she shook rattled a warning. She banged it against a large hip. "Oh, happy DAY!" she sang.

"Holy cow!" Ryan joked, and didn't bother to whisper. The music drowned out his words.

The girl's Labrador raised his muzzle, sniffing. The girl set her hand on his head to steady herself and the two stood in tableau. Abruptly the dog got off his haunches. Then the waiting moment broke, and everything happened at once.

Hannah heard scrabbling on the road behind her. Something hurled past and knocked her down.

"Bello! Heel!" Ethan yelled.

Bello barked as he frantically tried to worm his way through the dense hedge.

The dog by the girl's side was barking too, but he remained in place. The singers were deep in the joy of praise giving.

"Bello!" Ryan grabbed Bello's collar and dragged the dog away from the bushes. Bello scrabbled, whining.

On the other side of the hedge, the girl with the sunglasses held her dog by the collar as well.

Ethan disentangled Laura's sweater from where she was

pinned to the hedge branches and picked Hannah up off the ground. She was bleeding and her knees hurt.

"Run for it!" Dom urged, and the cousins scattered on the driveway. The Lab continued to bark. Voices began the next song. "If I had a hammer," they sang.

The cousins ran until they almost reached the Schroyer camp. Everyone except Dawn was out of breath; she had remained closest to the top of the driveway, poised to dash away. "I know better than to trust *any* outing with my brothers, especially one organized by Ryan," she commented. "Nice going, Squirt!"

"What a crazy group!" Ryan rolled his head back and forth and mimicked the singers.

Hannah stood uncertainly and didn't laugh. They were still shielded by the cover of the dark and the others couldn't see her. She was glad for once to feel invisible. Her cousins sang, but the off-key noise they made was silly in comparison to what she had heard at the retreat. She had spied on looks of pure happiness in the faces around the bonfire. Hannah wasn't at all sure what she'd just witnessed.

☐

Aunt Jeri and Aunt Lena were waiting for them when they got back to the cabin. Bello preceded them, tail wagging. "Good dog, Bello," Aunt Jeri praised. Bello shoved a moist muzzle into her hand for a milk bone treat. "It was getting late, so I sent the dog out to track you. You must have been pretty far down the road." None of the children commented, although only the youngest, Dom, managed to look totally innocent.

"Princess Rain Clouds, you're bleeding!" Aunt Lena exclaimed. "What in the world's happened to you?"

"I fell on the gravel," Hannah lied, and felt warmed by the looks of grateful complicity her cousins gave her.

"The unerring instinct to find trouble," Aunt Lena laughed, but her tone was gentle.

"Let me put some band aids on those. And it's almost time for sparklers." Aunt Jeri painted mercurochrome on each of Hannah's knees. "This will hurt when it sterilizes the cuts, Princess," she informed Hannah. "Your knees are going to be a funny color for a while."

Hannah was too fascinated by the garish hue of the mercurochrome to complain at the sting of it on her scratches.

When Aunt Jeri finished, everyone trooped to the lakefront. The adults had finished off plenty of beers and generated a good collection of six-pack yokes. Laughing as they worked, the unsober team of Uncle Aaron and Uncle Don transformed the clothesline. The children arrived as they draped the last plastic rings over the rope. "Everyone here? You kids all finally ready?" Uncle Aaron distributed sparklers and Uncle Don ignited them with his lit Bic.

The sparkler sticks sizzled as the children waved their arms. They filled the air with scrolls and arabesques. Curlicues of writing glowed and faded, and were covered over with more bright loops and squiggles.

When Uncle Don lit the beer rings an acrid smell rose. *Bjjzzt*. Eerie-colored blobs of burning plastic hissed and spit as they dripped from the clothesline. The grass shriveled where the molten plastic hit the ground. *Bjjzzt*, the beer rings sputtered, and psychedelic colors fell.

Hannah stood and watched, mesmerized by the pyrotechnics.

"Don't get too close," Uncle Don warned. "That plastic's hot. And it's going to leave one hell of a mess." He looked over to Hannah's parents. "It's not the bottle rockets Tammy said you were going to pick up, but this'll have to do."

"I told you," said Fred. "The fairgrounds fireworks stand was sold out." Maybe he was drunker than the others, because he stumbled over his explanation.

"Most likely you got too busy to pick them up." Don's voice was soft.

"Most likely." Fred drained the can of beer in his hand and reached over into the cooler for another. "A previous engagement. That's the way it goes."

Tammy sat beside Jeri and Lena, the women's faces careful blanks as they pretended not to understand.

"It goes that way a lot with you, doesn't it?" Uncle Don asked in the same soft voice.

"Dad, I need another sparkler. Mine went out!" Hannah tugged at Fred's arm.

"Sure, kiddo. They're right here." Fred turned away and busied himself with his daughter.

☐

Hannah woke the next morning to the sound of metallic notes. She lay in the dark, trying to remember where she was. Hannah had slept in a tent with Laura and Ethan to free up a cot in the cabin.

Ethan had staked it out far away from the others. The old pup tent was too small for three people. It was now so crowded that Laura and Ethan had no room to turn over without jostling Hannah, let alone do any messing around.

Hannah lay in a musty-smelling sleeping bag and listened to a bugle. *Gotta get up gotta get up gotta get up in the mo-o-o-r-ning* it called. The brassy sounds from over the lake carried in the morning air.

"God, what's that noise?" Laura stirred beside her and groaned.

Ethan moved in his sleeping bag. "The scout camp," he answered.

"A scout camp? First you drag me to spy on a religious retreat." Laura kept her voice low. "It's too early! It's still dark out."

Hannah started to roll on her left and the tent walls bowed alarmingly.

Ethan yawned. "There's a Boy Scout camp at the other end of the lake. Our summertime at Crystal Lake overlaps with theirs. We get to wake up at the crack of dawn just like they do. They use a real bugle player; it's not a tape. He stands at the edge of the water and plays as loud as he can, so it carries on the water. Echo effect," Ethan ended thoughtfully. Hannah recognized the pedantic note that crept into his voice. After all, he *was* a Schroyer.

☐

Two days later, before breakfast, Dom, Hannah, Laura, and Ethan walked back to the retreat. Hannah had repeatedly begged to go; she wanted a look at it in the daylight. For the last two nights she had lain in the tent with hymns echoing in the space between her ears. It gave her the creeps. Stubborn, she wanted to know why.

"What's that? Do you hear that?" Her feet slowed as they reached the retreat center driveway.

The air was literally humming. "Om, mani padme hum," she heard.

Ethan cocked his head, listening. "The fourth of July yoga and meditation retreat. Sounds like they're doing the chanting portion."

"Can you see them?" whispered Hannah. She moved around to Ethan's left and gripped his free hand. Hannah shrank against his side, wishing she could make herself invisible again.

"How come you're whispering?" Laura's normal tone sounded far too loud.

The four of them placed themselves alongside the hedges and peered through the branches at the prayer center. In the daylight everything was easier to make out.

Hannah stared at the stained-glass windowpanes. She could identify two black-and-white paisley forms with dots; a skinny sickle moon and a five-pointed star; a six-pointed yellow star that was made of two triangles; Jesus holding out palms that had holes in them.

A new, smaller group of worshippers sat cross legged on cushions on the platform. Each held a small bowl or a drum. "Om, mani padme hum." Ting. Ting. Boom. A clear ringing sound followed each phrase as people struck the sides of metal bowls with little wooden sticks and quietly pounded drums. The clang of the struck bowls reverberated in the morning.

"Ommmm, mani padme hummmm."

"What does that even mean?" Hannah's gaze moved to the next panels and she grew more perplexed. The window panels represented an old bearded man who had wings, standing next to a beast that was both lion and eagle; an outstretched palm, with a wheel in the middle of it; a man sitting cross-legged on top of a pink lotus as a cobra snake spread its hood over his head; a man with the head of an elephant, also sitting cross-legged.

As if she'd read her mind, the woman leading the chanters spoke. "You've just recited 'Hail to the jewel in the lotus.' It's the mantra of the Buddha of Compassion, the goddess Guan Yin. Her mantra calms fears and heals broken hearts. Let's keep going with the next one. Om ah hum vajra guru padma siddhi hum."

"Om ah hum vajra guru padma siddhi hum."

"Ommmm ah hum vajra guru padma siddhi hummmm."

"Hannah?"

She jumped at the sound of her name.

In the middle of the driveway stood the heavyset girl from two nights ago. Someone had braided her hair and a blond plait hung down her back. She wore a loose print shift and the same dark glasses. The small black Labrador accompanied her, its tail wagging slowly back and forth.

"Hannah?" The girl took a few steps towards them, the dog on its special leash leading.

"How do you know my name?" Hannah squeaked.

"It's my name, too," the girl remarked calmly. "You got here a few days ago, didn't you?"

"Hannah!" The new voice was both deep and shrill, and definitely dreadful. "Hannah, get back over here! Leave the neighbor kids alone!" The beefy woman who had played the tambourine waddled into the driveway. Her neck was an alarming shade of red and today she was holding a lawn rake in her hand.

"That's my mother," the blind girl said. "I have to go. Come by tomorrow if you want to talk. I get feelings sometimes, and I have one with you. You'll get special luck," said the blind girl. The dog, its tail still wagging ever so slightly, turned and led her away.

Hannah's face was wet as she led them swiftly from the retreat.

"Why aren't we heading back to the cabin? And why are you crying?" Dom looked at Ethan and Laura, and again at his cousin.

Tears dripped from Hannah's nose. "How does she know my name?" she asked tremulously. "If she's blind, how did she know I was there? No one *ever* sees me, but she did. And what did she mean, special luck? Is that good, or is it bad?"

Dom and Laura looked at her uneasily.

"She's blind, she's not deaf and dumb, Hannah. They must know we have a place on the same road, because her mother told her to leave the neighbor kids alone." Ethan rubbed her shoulders. "And Hannah's a special name."

"I hate that name!" sobbed Princess Rain Clouds.

From the trees overhead the approaching rain pattered on leaves and trunks, and it began to pour. Hannah was soaked by the time they got back to the cabin.

□

The storm squall passed over Crystal Lake as quickly as it had blown in. Only the plops of rain dripping from the crowns of trees gave proof of how hard it had rained. When the wind blew, water drummed in short bursts on the pitched roof of the cabin.

That afternoon the kids played cards out on the porch. When the cousins visited, they always played several games simultaneously. Ryan, Ethan, Dawn and Dom teamed up for hearts. The others played gin rummy. Jake was in the living room with the adults, talking to Uncle Aaron about a job on the construction crew. After Laura lost the first two hands, she removed herself from the games to sulk on the cot against the fireplace's back wall.

Hannah kept winning, and she smiled. Without her brother there to censor her, she could savor beating them and carry on a running commentary on her cousins' poor plays. "Boy, what a bad move!" she scoffed as she scooped up cards. Hannah freely included all her cousins in her remarks. But they had thick skins; she needed to work to puncture the Schroyer family self-confidence. This sense of security was what Hannah most wanted to breach – and to be included in.

The bugle from the Boy Scout camp sounded as the sun vanished below the hazy horizon. It started raining again. *Day is done, gone the sun, from the lakes, from the hills, from the sky. All is well, safely rest, God is nigh.*

Hannah was still enjoying a winning streak when she heard a rustling sound. "Rocky's awake!" She dropped her cards and ran over to the corner where the flying squirrel had emerged from his nest. Each evening she waited excited for the creature to wake up. The others crowded around the cage behind her. Hannah refused to let anyone get in front of her. Rocky was the most wonderful animal she had ever seen.

"Everybody move back," Dom ordered. He and Dawn were responsible for cleaning the cage, and this meant they were the ones allowed to take Rocky in and out of it. Obediently everyone stepped away. Dom lifted the lid to the cage, and Dawn reached inside.

Rocky was ready for her hands; he climbed up her arm and leapt from there onto the porch screen windows. With another leap he landed on one of the shelves erected for him on the fireplace wall. A nest had been prepared and the squirrel liked the location because of the warmth from the bricks, just like the kids did.

Dawn went back inside the cabin. Ethan took Laura's hand and led her outside. Everyone else stayed still, watching as a soft creature that weighed less than a pound leapt confidently around the air in the long porch. Rocky launched himself into space with his limbs spread wide. When the flying squirrel flew his skin stretched taut, like the membranes that bats used to fly over the cabin, or the sails that propelled boats across the lake.

For fifteen minutes the cousins barely spoke. Hannah watched the squirrel with her mouth hanging open.

Ethan and Laura had vanished, but Dawn returned to the porch with a bowl of sunflower seeds and nuts. "Rocky's excited, but give him time and he'll come back down. Maybe tonight's the night he'll eat out of your hand." She doled out food to her cousins and they took expectant places around the porch.

Dawn laid a line of seeds along the window ledge. Rocky flew back to the screen and hanging on to it with his claws he made his way towards the food.

"Over here, Princess." Dawn pulled her cousin's arm until she stood sideways at the screen. Dawn set Hannah's hand against the ledge. Gently she pried Hannah's fingers open to expose the seeds she was clutching. "Don't move."

Hannah didn't. As Rocky came closer she could barely breathe. The squirrel's claws snicked against her skin as it climbed into her palm. Rocky sat on his haunches and, front paws holding a seed, began to eat. The other kids saw the expression on Hannah's face and didn't clamor to take her place. Instead, everyone watched Rocky as he ate from Hannah's hand. It was, in a summer filled with too much rain, Hannah's first moment of true happiness.

☐

When it was time for bed, the kids bickered over who would get the cot on the porch and who had to use the tents.

"I want the porch cot!" Dom whined.

"I want to sleep next to the fireplace! It's my turn tonight!" Dawn insisted.

Hannah walked to Ethan's tent as usual. This evening it was zipped tight. When she began to open it, a hand shot out and held her by the wrist.

"Stay right there, Princess," Ethan suggested. "It's better if tonight you find somewhere else to sleep."

In the tent Laura murmured something.

"No! Just us tonight," said Ethan, and he zipped the tent flaps closed again.

Hannah stood uncertainly in the wet yard for a few minutes before going back to the cabin. The others were still arguing about sleeping spots.

She headed for the spare bedroom without telling anyone. No one liked to sleep in that bedroom; the mattresses were too hard, and the room walls didn't reach all the way to the ceiling.

Hannah crawled into the bedsheets of the top bunk. She lay in bed listening to adult voices float over from the living room. She could see the cord of the lamp that hung in the kitchen. It created a long and surprisingly wide shadow, slanting across her bed. Hours later she woke to the muted bang of a door closing as the adults headed for their own tents.

Only two voices still murmured; it was extremely late. The voices came closer.

"Hey Fred, just a sec. Need to talk to you. You see, word is you don't do driving runs alone these days."

*His voice is all blurry*, Hannah thought.

"I don't know what you're talking about," answered her father.

"No? Come in the kitchen," the first voice suggested.

Hannah turned, uneasy, trying to fall back to sleep. The bunk bed was flush against the dividing wall, and when the first hard thud came from the other side it felt to Hannah like that thud was smashing into her bones.

Whump

"What the hell?"

Whump

"Your daughter Hannah's a sweet, sweet, sad little girl," the other voice slurred. "She's a little princess, and you're a royal asshole!"

As frightened as she was, when she heard herself being described she needed to see. Hannah stood on the bed. The cord of the kitchen lamp jumped up, black against grainy white. It swung to the right and fell again.

She got on her tiptoes and looked over the flimsy wood of the dividing wall. Hannah looked down at grotesquely oversized shadows, slamming their foreheads together. Her father and Uncle Don hugged one another hard as their fists thumped.

"You plan on taking *Laura* for a drive?"

"Son of a bitch!" Fred's breath rasped in pain.

Don cursed in a steady flow of words between blows. "You're a loser, you're such a piece of shit, God I hate you,

you just never stop lying Fred, do you? You destroy anything you come in contact with, my sister deserves better, you don't deserve her or your kids. And, Ethan's girlfriend? Seriously? Could you be any slimier?"

Don slammed Fred against the stove.

Whump

"Yeah? I hate you too," Fred panted. "Don and the superior Schroyers. I hate all of you!"

They lurched back and forth between the cabinets and walls and banged hard into the table. Don slammed into another wall and her father's right elbow hit the wood with hard sharp bang.

Whump

The swinging lamp hit a kitchen cabinet and shattered. The cabin pitched into darkness. Thuds continued and glass crunched as the men rolled about. Hannah stared into gray, unable to breathe.

Ten minutes later a door slammed, and the high beams of a car reflected on the cabin windows. An engine started, and the car drove away.

☐

Hannah looked curiously at Uncle Don. Her uncle had a cloth band wrapped around his forehead, held there with a rainbow-colored safety pin from one of Ricky's diapers. His skin was flushed, partly from the bag of ice cubes under the cloth.

"Did you cut your head on that light bulb last night when it got smashed?"

"Yeah, you could say that, Princess." Uncle Don tried to smile, but his head hurt.

Hannah persisted. "Why were you rolling on the floor in the kitchen? What were you and my dad fighting about?"

"Hannah, you weren't watching over the top of the wall,

were you?" Alarmed, Uncle Don looked at Hannah through eyes swollen from drinking, or tears.

"Yes, and every time you bumped the wall between me and the kitchen I could feel it. You were loud!"

"Sometimes adults drink more than they should and then they say and do dumb things."

"Even you?"

The screen door squeaked, and Uncle Don and Hannah turned. Tammy stood on the threshold. She crossed the room and picked up her daughter. Tammy's red-rimmed eyes looked over her head at Uncle Don. "Your uncle is a great guy, Hannah. He's the best little brother I could have asked for. If you're lucky, you'll grow up and marry someone just like him." Her voice broke and Tammy hugged Hannah tighter. Hannah tried not to squirm; her mother never picked her up anymore. Finally, Tammy set Hannah back on her feet, but kept one arm firmly around her shoulders. *Why is Mom hugging me so tight?* Hannah wondered.

Uncle Don turned around, his left arm wrapped around Tammy's shoulder. His right hand held the ice against his temple. Hannah thought that the ice had melted because her uncle's face had suddenly grown wet.

The door opened again, and Aunt Lena came in the room. Hannah was sure she would ask why they were hugging each other so tightly. But Lena went directly to Uncle Don and put her arms around him, too.

She gently stroked her husband's temple. Uncle Don hugged her close and lay his head against his wife's. "Sometimes I act so stupid I surprise even myself," he murmured into Aunt Lena's hair.

Everyone sent meaningful looks to one another over Hannah's head. Uncle Aaron and Aunt Jeri entered the room. They had been standing in the doorway watching silently.

"The car's still gone. Fred didn't come back."

"No loss," said Uncle Aaron.

Uncle Don spoke up. "Tam, you can ride with us. And the kids can ride with Ethan and Laura."

"Thank the Lord for SUVs," Aunt Lena added.

☐

Lena and Don gave Tammy a lift home. Ethan and Laura followed in Ethan's car with Hannah and Jake in the back seat.

Hannah cried the entire trip. "I have to go talk with the other Hannah before we go!" She was almost hysterical with frustration and grief. "But why can't I go talk to her?" she kept sobbing.

The Podolski car wasn't in the driveway when they pulled in. "Why isn't Dad home?" Hannah kept asking. "If he didn't drive back with us, where's Dad?" Hannah was baffled that her father disappeared with the family automobile.

With difficulty, Tammy tried to explain to Jake and Hannah where their father went. "Mom, I'm sixteen," Jake reminded her. "I have a good idea of exactly where he went. I've overheard Dad on his cell phone more than once."

"But he drives trucks," Hannah insisted. "Why did he take the car to go somewhere?"

She had nightmares for the next few weeks. Something happened to her at the lake; it was all mixed up in unseeing sight, and fighting adults, and hymns and the drone of chants. Some mornings she woke from a dream of a bugle blowing. No matter how hard she tried, Hannah could never recall if the song was Reveille or Taps.

She was terrified. Her luck had been decided, and she was afraid to look in its direction. She might be doomed to stay invisible forever. Why wasn't she allowed to go back and talk with the other Hannah? It was like the blind girl could see everything. If Princess Rain Clouds had asked, that Hannah would have explained what was happening to her. She had lost her chance to ask, and now it was too late.

At Thanksgiving Tammy cooked a holiday dinner, just for her and the kids and Fred. "Can we try again?" he asked, and Tammy agreed.

Princess Rain Clouds took the omens and checked her luck. It was an unusually mild autumn, but she was worried.

Inevitably, the weather always turned cold.

# Do Dreams Float?

Paul's training had come to an abrupt halt when his appendix burst. Just as abruptly, he and Libby eloped.

Mondo© Racing Bikes spun the story of their favorite mascot into a marketing coup. Paul Capriolo, the company's sponsored Ironman, was taking a break from training to marry a beautiful Asian-African American artist. For a week their website posted a photo of Paul with his wife. More amused than annoyed when he saw the notice, Paul insisted that they remove it.

Paul and Libby honeymooned at Lake Como. The locals adored the American athlete who spoke flawless Italian and had an attractive woman at his side. The newlyweds remained at the lake and rented a room in a hotel villa frequented by Europeans. The marble foyer was always cool, and the building had a long lawn facing the lake. Their little second floor room was affordable, and its balcony gave them a dreamy view of the water. The gauze curtains in the tall windows caught the lake's breezes.

Paul endured the break in training to heal, then resumed his grueling regimen for coming competitions. Their days settled into a rhythm and June and July passed swiftly. He ran and biked the winding roads and swam the lake. Libby sketched, inspired by the region's beauty.

One day they ate lunch and afterwards made love. Libby came back out of the bathroom; Paul was still lounging on the bed.

Light streamed through the curtains, and from where she stood the bed with Paul in it seemed to float. "Don't get up," Libby ordered. Reflexively Paul moved to pull the sheet back over his body. "I want to capture this light! Don't move."

She pulled the sheet to the bottom of the bed. Paul grinned and stretched out among the pillows. The sun's rays cast parallel bars of light across his stomach. Libby grabbed the nearest sketchbook and drew rapidly. Even his appendectomy scar was beautiful.

When she finished her preliminary sketches and set down the drawing pad, Paul showered and got ready for his afternoon workout. He was on a winning streak, finishing first or second in every race he entered. The enforced rest after the appendectomy had been beneficial. Paul had returned to competitions with fresh energy and focus and the happiness of a newly married man.

"How many kilometers to go?" she asked.

"This week?" He pulled on swimming trunks and tallied aloud. "Three hundred K cycling, check. A hundred K running. Check. I'll finish the week's thirty kilometers of swimming today."

Libby laughed. She was giddy from good sex and a promising set of new drawings. "No rest for the wicked. Athletes are insane. Don't you ever get tired of it?"

"No. I love racing! It was a pain in the ass to have to stop and heal. Although I liked the honeymoon! But, scale back or train less?" Paul kissed her hard and considered a minute before he continued. "Swim, run, bike…. Each puts different demands on the body. It's really not about technique. Actually, it's not even the race that matters."

"So, what is it?"

"Being ready, mentally and physically. It's doing the hard work and getting up and training, every, single, day. I push myself beyond where people are willing to go. That fact gives me the most pride of all."

"And I get the benefit of your hard work." Laughing, she ran appreciative hands across his torso.

Paul left, and Libby sat out on the balcony to work on the

sketches. She knew he would be gone for at least four hours. Her limbs still languid, she went in for a nap. She woke from a dream in which her husband floated naked in bed, on a lake.

Libby changed into a summer dress and went back out on the balcony. It was almost five o'clock and she'd spot him crossing the lawn when he returned from his swim.

He would be hungry. Paul ate phenomenally large portions at every meal. He charmed the local restaurants by swearing their food for supper each night made him a winner. "Left on my own, food doesn't matter," he informed them. "I follow the see food, eat food diet. It's just fuel. But here? Madonna, I live for these meals. There's nothing better than Italian cooking."

At six-thirty, Paul hadn't returned. Libby suspected he was trapped in another conversation about where in the north his grandparents came from, and how that made his heritage Swiss rather than Italian. She strolled down to the lakefront to rescue him.

She spotted his cargo pants and shirt folded on a large blue and white striped towel on the shore. He was surely still in his bathing suit, chatting as people appreciated his physique. She collected the clothes and walked from shop to shop, asking if anyone had seen Paul. She cursed her inability to speak the language. "He went swimming," she said as she breast-stroked the air.

But everyone knew Paolo, and they shook their heads, no, they hadn't seen him.

Libby spent a fruitless hour searching. When she returned to the hotel there was still no sign of him. She ate dinner in the hotel, sitting where she could watch the foyer. When the dining room closed, Libby admitted to herself that the situation was grave.

"My husband's missing," she informed the front desk. She sat in the foyer as they waited for the police, her hand circling the new wedding band around and around her finger. Libby endured the curious stares of patrons sitting in the hotel bar where they could simultaneously drink and watch the street.

A trio of police officers arrived half an hour later. "Let's do this somewhere private, sí?" the manager was kind enough to suggest. He accompanied Libby and the policemen to her room and translated as Libby explained the situation.

"My husband went for a swim this afternoon and didn't come back. No, he went alone. What do I do? I'm an artist. Yes, everything was fine. When I last saw him? Tell them, today at lunch. I sketched and later on I took a nap. Yes, I often take afternoon naps."

"Permesso," the police said.

"They want to see your drawings," the manager explained.

Libby blushed as she handed over the portfolio. The three policemen examined each one of her nude studies of Paul and turned to her with courteous smiles. "Che belli," one of them nodded. But they wished to keep the portfolio. Their faces were solemn as they made the next request. "Do you have a current photograph of your husband?"

Libby hesitated, considering which photograph was the most recent. She handed them a glossy publicity still of Paul crossing the finish line at the July marathon in Milan. The police officer who took it from her looked at the photograph and exclaimed. He handed it to his colleagues and they passed it from man to man, all talking at once.

"What are they saying?" Libby waited for them to finish, anxious as she looked to the manager for clarity.

"Signora, they say they are shocked to know that the missing foreigner is Paolo Capriolo, the triathlete. All of them saw the end of the race on the news reports and remember the story of the Italian American who won the Milano marathon!" Nodding, the police officers touched the photograph in confirmation. They conferred with the manager, who turned back to her. "The authorities have to wait forty-eight hours to report someone as a missing person. But he was going for a swim, and Paolo is a public figure. They will do what they can to speed up the search."

Libby waited in limbo. Interpol had no leads to his disappearance and neither did the police stations around the lake. She woke on the fourth morning in a sticky daze. The same dream faded, Paul floating. Groggy, she heard the jangle of the telephone by the window. She jumped out of the bed to grab it.

"Signora Capriolo?" a male voice asked.

"Hello? Yes? Uh, I mean, sí!" Libby put conviction in her answer, because she was a missus, she was still a married woman unless events proved otherwise.

"My apologies for disturbing you. Can you be downstairs in thirty minutes? We have information about your husband. Our man will find you on the patio."

Her knee joints turned to rubber. "I'll be right there." Someone had news about Paul, but they didn't have Paul himself. Her heart was thudding so hard she had to sit on the edge of the bed until her dizziness passed. She dressed swiftly and clutched her purse and room key close to her chest. In the hallway she pushed the button for the elevator; without waiting for it to arrive Libby took the stairs. She was moving so fast she almost fell as she reached the next landing. Her brain pounded, terror and hope both fighting for her attention.

When she entered the patio the other hotel guests swiveled in their seats and stared. Libby was never sure if she stood out because she was a beautiful woman, or if the Italians stared at her for being part black and part Korean. She'd spent her entire life in a heightened state of self-conscious awareness; it didn't matter if the lingering glances were prejudice about her skin color or desire for her gorgeous features. Being scrutinized had been a part of her identity for as far back as she could recall.

This morning they put their heads together over their breakfasts to whisper, and one man even pointed a discreet finger.

*That's the donna with the missing husband.*

*We saw her, four days ago. She was waiting with the manager and then three carabinieri showed up, red lights flashing.*

*Surely you heard the news about the famous triathlete Paolo Capriolo?*

*They're on an extended holiday.*

*I was told, they eloped.*

*No, he was in training for the next Ironman and suddenly he vanished.*

*I heard he got second thoughts about being married to a black woman.*

*No, supposedly she's mostly Asian. Japanese, they say.*

*I heard he was hit by a car while biking.*

*I heard he was hit by a car while out on a run, such a tragedy.*

*I heard he met someone else and abandoned her.*

*I heard he took up with a starlet, or was it he reunited with that Olympic gold medalist swimmer?*

*I heard they're dragging the lake.*

No one spoke loudly enough for her to hear, but she could imagine the remarks. Libby had tormented herself, thinking and fearing the comments, dreading all those scenarios since the afternoon Paul disappeared.

The maître de led Libby to a table on the lawn. A waiter came to her at once with a glass of fresh orange juice and a cup of American coffee. He held out a menu with a questioning look; she shook her head. He left, and she gazed unseeing at the grass. She became dizzy again and rested her head on her forearms. Libby whispered quietly to herself as she took shallow breaths. Please still be alive. Please still be alive. Please still be alive.

The sunlight vanished. "Signora?"

Libby looked up, and a shadow covered her where she shrank back against the chair cushions. The largest man she had ever seen blocked her view of the lake. His face was defined by a carefully clipped pointed beard and short curly hair so dark it shimmered. His physical presence contained a weight solid enough to ground the lawn, the lake, all of northern Italy to the chair where she cowered. She peered up, struck dumb as she waited for his news.

He just stood there, immovable as a mountain.

"I'm so sorry," she apologized, but she wasn't sure why. Libby needed to think what to do next. She pointed at the chair next to her. "Please, sit."

First he set the items she lent the police on the table and her husband smiled at her from the photo. She stared: was this going to be the last photo of Paul ever taken?

The big man seated himself, leaned forward, and touched her elbow. He could crush her with his hand, with a look, with whatever was about to come out of his mouth. Libby knew, with a horrid certainty, he was going to say those words.

"I have news. You must be strong. We have learned that this man" – he tapped Paul's face – "is dead. Your husband drowned. A group from Belarus rented a ski boat last week. A boy was on the skis; his father was steering the boat. And they ignored the flag your husband had attached to himself, the international warning sign that someone is in the water and vessels need to watch out. The boy on skis ran right over him. The boat did not come back to see if Paolo needed help. I am told, the Belarussians left town that night. They did not even have time to return the boat. They left it tied to a dock; it had to be towed back. The skis have gone missing.

"It took until last night before witnesses came forward." His expression was stony as the air on the patio gathered and thickened. "This morning at dawn, divers recovered Paolo's body. He was struck on the head by both of the skis; if the boat had gone back for him, maybe he could have survived his injuries."

He lifted Libby's right hand where it trembled in her lap and held it tightly. When he removed his own hand, a folded slip of paper lay in her palm. "For later," he said, and his dark eyes glittered. "For the time when you want to know justice. We cannot bring your Paolo back. But signora, dial this number and say his name followed by the word yes, and a certain family won't ever return for a vacation."

Libby was trembling so hard that her whole body quivered.

The expression in his eyes softened and became human again. "Paolo was like a son to us. He brought honor to our town. He made us proud. It's not right someone good should simply, vanish, sink beneath the waves like a stone, forgive my clichés but there is no way to explain." The big man signaled, and the waiter brought an espresso. He drank it in one swallow, set the tiny cup back on the tray. "A translator by the name of D'Angelo will get in touch with you to take care of all the police details." But he didn't give Libby his own name or say if he was from the police.

He picked her shaking hand back up and curled her fingers around that slip of paper. "A phone call and justice is done," he repeated. He rose to his feet. "We hope you stay on for as long as you need to, as long as you want to. It was our great pleasure to host you and sincere sorrow that Paolo died on this spot."

"We were happy here. He loves Italy. Loved. I love it too," she sobbed. Libby reached blindly into her purse for a tissue. By the time she could stop crying and looked back up, the lake glimmered and the stranger was nowhere to be seen. She returned the sodden tissue to her purse. Underneath, in the front pocket, she tucked the phone number.

Libby stayed on at the lake, unable to leave yet. The hotel

displayed one of Paul's glossy photographs in the lobby with a lit candle and fresh flowers that they changed each day. She endured the sympathy of the other hotel guests, who approached one by one to speak to her and give their condolences. Libby went into the town as little as possible.

The days that followed were a succession of necessary gruesome details. When she was taken to identify Paul's body, she couldn't bring herself to look at his mangled face. Instead, she identified him by the appendectomy scar, a tender red that would never fade now. There was an autopsy. The police handed her a death certificate to sign. She filled out paperwork to have his body flown home.

She wrapped the folded note in plastic and placed it in the small alabaster box Paul had bought for her on their honeymoon. She always kept it close. But she didn't open it; she'd already memorized the phone number. The single time she saw it, the digits seared themselves onto her retinas.

Libby was paralyzed. Her life became as glassy and slippery as the surface of his photo, of Lake Como. Details swam up, and details sank. The feel of Paul's body, the plans they made, that last lunch they ate together: images arrived suddenly and washed her in a threat of sorrow, and, just as abruptly, vanished.

She could barely recall that last afternoon when she drew Paul in the floating bed. Those Lake Como sketches! Had she created signposts to the trail of events that landed her, ended him, here?

A boat had killed Paul and simply sped on by.

Libby was an artist, but she was incapable of delineating her grief. The world had lost its contours, and what could she do to prevent further blurring? She clung to her remaining memories, buoyed by a photograph of her husband smiling at her.

The big man dominated her impressions of that fateful afternoon. His figure blocked out events. He loomed, and she clung to his image hoping it could continue to block everything else. She still heard the steel in his voice, suggesting she make a call and snuff out the guilty. That, she remembered. Something was just a phone call away... but it wasn't Paul.

She woke each morning from the dream of Paul floating in a bed on the lake. Each time, Libby took out the folded piece of paper and held it in her palm for protection. She would dial that number, and someone would murder the people responsible for her husband's death. Before they died, would the cowards know why? Would the big man do the job himself?

How she wished *she* were a trained assassin. She imagined ninja training. She pictured herself as she blotted out and defaced their existences. And this: she imagined them, defaced. In other fantasies, an implacable Libby forced them off a remote road in a country she could neither find on a map nor name a single town in. During terrible dark nights when she woke sobbing, Libby's visions filled with the righteousness of revenge.

The pain of loss was coming for her, and she was in no hurry to meet its debilitating forces. Hers was a marathon of delayed grief, a discipline that gave shape to all her waking hours. She willed herself to remain numb. She needed to prepare.

"It's doing the hard work," Paul had told her, "getting up and training, every, single, day. To push beyond where people are willing to go." She recalled his words as her memories slipped away. The dream of Paul was all that remained. Why? Libby wondered. Do dreams float? She ached for an answer.

Do dreams float?

## The Green Under the Snow

The hunter flexed his shoulders in the green plaid jacket he wore under an orange hunting vest. It was snowing harder and time to head back to the lodge. He stood, and suddenly there was the telltale whoosh of birds flying from their hiding place. A shot rang out from somewhere close.

The hunter began walking and saw a pink stain on the snow. What the…. Something felt wrong. Was he bleeding? He put a hand over his stomach and when he pulled the hand away his glove was stained crimson.

He *was* bleeding. He bent over, suddenly dizzy, and almost fell. Someone had shot him.

He staggered to the shelter of a tall pine. When he reached it he dropped, slumping heavily against the tree trunk, and the world faded to white.

☐

Luisa left for work earlier than usual. It was a long walk from the housing project where she and her relatives lived. Snowplow crews were working to keep the main road in and out of town cleared and drivable. They would get to the secondary roads later, and no one cleared the trail in the woods that the locals took. The hike to her job at the Lodge usually took her forty minutes. In the ongoing storm the trail might be hard to see.

"Be careful! Keep an eye out for the hunters! And don't leave the path to the Lodge! Be careful!" her uncle kept repeating.

Her aunt made Luisa wear the brightest-colored shawl

they owned between the two of them. She bundled Luisa in three sweaters and an orange vest and wrapped the shawl with a pattern of red and purple flowers over her shoulders. "You look like an exotic bird. Hopefully, you don't get shot," her uncle said, cupping her cheeks.

When she left the apartment, Luisa was grateful for the extra layers of clothes. She had never gotten used to the cold.

The skies were the color of the local stone. Slate: a quiet gray that enveloped rather than threatened. Fat snowflakes fell in spirals. Luisa could just hear the hushed landing of snow on the ground all around her.

People at home swore that the north was cold, the food was cold, the way of life was cold, and the gringos were frío. Those things might all be true, but Luisa loved the unexpected abundance of the land. She looked in wonder at the forest she walked through, nothing like home. Snow created a mantle sparkling inside with frozen crystals. And underneath that mantle were more shades of natural green than she had ever imagined existed. It might be winter, but even this place, deep in the woods, contained green trees, and shrubs, and bushes, and plants in the snow with bright red berries. Used to the sunshine of her southern country, Luisa was deeply thrilled by all the plants alive and even suited to freezing weather.

For the last decade she had lived with her aunt and uncle. Luisa worked at the local resort and sent money home to her mother every month. She had progressed from the simple tasks of making beds and cleaning rooms to her current position as the Head of Housekeeping.

She clocked the most hours, responsible for the roster of young men and women employed at the lodge. The owner recognized her intelligence and work ethic. He helped her enroll in online bookkeeping classes. Luisa pored slowly over English-language textbooks and presented him with a five-year plan. She had, he assured her in Spanglish, a mucho buena future.

Now, a heavy gust blew snow in her face and Luisa shivered. The winds battered her slender form. The vista was white for as far as her gaze could penetrate in the pale light. White, white, white. Where was the green of the vegetation? She spotted a splotch of color in the woods up ahead.

She brought a mittened hand to her forehead and squinted. A shotgun was propped against a pine tree. Beside it was a plaid green pile with red patches and neon orange. It was almost invisible under a layer of snow.

She heard her steady breaths as she plodded through the snowdrifts. Luisa knelt. "Ai!" she gasped, her voice lost in the wind. Luisa bit into the mitten covering her right hand and pulled it off with her teeth. She wiped snow from the man's face. He opened his eyes, but she wasn't sure he saw her. She fumbled the knitted mitten back over her cold fingers.

"Mister, you think you can walk? We're close to the lodge, just a little further on the trail. Maybe ten minutes."

The hunter mumbled and closed his eyes again. Luisa couldn't make out his words. "Mister!" she said louder. She took off the shawl and wrapped it around his head, tying the ends firmly under his chin. "You stand up!" She grasped at his arms and both were surprised by her strength.

She wrestled him upright, using the bole of the tree to take his weight. Once she had him on his feet Luisa pulled his arm over her shoulder. "You're hurt! Help me, you got to walk a little!"

He took a step and moaned as the pain woke him up. He opened his eyes, then stared at the angel assisting him. Her raven hair was flecked with flakes of snow.

The angel kept up a steady flow of conversation. "We'll come back later for your gun. I can't carry you both. That's a bad wound you got there. You need a doctor for sure. But I think it's to the belly, and that's where people always bleed real bad. Back at home, when I was little, my brother, Javi, he got stuck on some barbed wire with the rabbit coops one year. He barely bled at all even though the wire cut him pretty deep. Mámmi said it was because he's such a skinny little kid, but I knew it was because he'd managed to stick himself in a big muscle. Plus the wire only got in so far, and you know bullets, mister, sí, it was a bullet, yes? Pues, bullets, they can go a long way before they stop, and you are a big guy, so there must be a lot of blood.

"Don't look at it, just keep walking, you're doing great. Mister, look up! We're almost there." The man moved a tiny bit faster when she added the fib. Luisa had no idea how near or how far away the lodge was. She lowered her own head and doggedly put one foot in front of the other as she tried to go on bearing the big man's weight. Where was the path?

He shambled, in a slogging rhythm that carried them along. The hunter heard her words from a far side of the chasm widening somewhere inside. He moved, encased in a soft bubble washed with flashes of incredible pain. The shawl around his head protected his eyes and ears and he was grateful to the girl for wrapping him in it; he had lost his cap. His feet and hands no longer felt attached to the rest of his body, and he was lightheaded, blood still leaking from his middle. How long had he slumped underneath the tree, waiting to die? Minutes? Hours?

The skies dimmed as the storm blotted out the final lingering bits of light. Luisa and the hunter stumbled on in the growing darkness. Ironically, the early darkness saved them. Sensors activated earlier than ever before. As lights clicked on in the dusk, the lodge lit up and they spotted the back of the building. The roof's turrets showed in sharp profile against the curtains of falling snow. The hunter groaned and collapsed to the ground. Luisa crawled across the back lawn, dragging him behind her.

Her boss, worrying over the need for candles and flashlights, looked out the kitchen windows and saw the humped form of a yeti approaching. But the yeti was wearing a brightly colored shawl that could only belong to Luisa.

He rushed to the back door, pushed it open against a snowdrift, and helped Luisa carry the hunter inside.

☐

They removed the hunter's wet clothes, disinfected and taped his gunshot wound with gauze, and covered him in wool blankets. The cook found an ID and hunting license wrapped in plastic in a pocket, along with the keys to a vehicle. Luisa's boss called the hospital in the city and described the condition of Mr. Eric Schott. "S C H O T T. Schott," he repeated.

"Heck of a name for a shooting victim," the cook muttered. Everyone laughed, relieved that Luisa was safe, and the hunter was going to live.

She sat at the kitchen table holding onto a mug of coffee laced with brandy. "Drink this. All of it," her boss ordered. "God help us if you have hypothermia too."

Luisa needed all her concentration to lift the mug without spilling it. She still trembled, but not from the cold. Luisa was realizing what had just happened.

☐

She lost her way in a snowstorm.
Someone shot a man and left the scene of the shooting.
She found him.
She saved that man's life.

☐

She had gotten involved.

The incident would be reported to the authorities. The policía would interview everyone. A request would become a demand to see identification papers and legal documents. Which she did not really have because Luisa was an illegal alien, and most of her papers were fake.

Her tía and tío, the aunt and uncle who had treated her like she was their own daughter since she had made her way north? What would happen to them when the story flew out? What would happen to her trusting, unsuspecting employer? And, Luisa herself? She would be punished. Maybe she'd be deported.

*I don't care*, Luisa thought, and drained her mug. Her boss promptly refilled it and poured himself another big swig of brandy too. She repeated the words silently. *I don't care!*

And then Luisa shook her head at herself. *I do care.* She hadn't for one second considered leaving the hunter in the woods to die. Luisa had always known this world is the trajectory of intersecting lives. When you see someone on your path who needs help, you help.

She drank the brandy. What came next didn't matter.

"Where did you find the strength to carry him?" Her boss looked at her in wonder.

She shrugged, feeling warmed. "When I found him there in the woods, I was lost. But I had to try."

"And you weren't scared you'd both freeze to death? How could you be so brave?"

"Well," she said. "Well, I believe it's like this, señor. You, me, everyone, we're the green under the snow."

# The Trail Back Out

### I: Prelude: Rain and Fire

Each evening, while twilight shadows lengthened, Ken sat and stared into the fire. What a shame it had taken what felt like the end of the world for him to return to the Adirondacks.

Ken had been working on the oil fracking fields and living in a container. The evenings consisted of lengthy monologues from men alternately bored, or angry, or scared, arguing over every subject with a captive audience.

Why aren't there any solitary quarters, he'd thought more than once. When a new wave of the mutated virus arrived, the corporation went into lockdown. All workers would quarantine with them or leave.

Ken looked around and couldn't imagine sharing a room with any of the men for an extended period. He stopped at the head office to quit and collected his back pay. Ken gathered his things (simultaneously relieved and strangely distressed that they made a small bundle) and drove away.

He traveled cross country, always heading east, not yet quite sure where he was going. In some places he took temporary work; no matter where he stayed, in his free hours Ken helped register people to vote. Outside Kansas City he bought camping gear and stocked the trunk of his car with canned goods and nonperishables.

His internal compass pointed its needle at his personal true north. When he pulled into Cranberry Lake township in upstate New York months later, Ken's eyes burned. He passed signs that stated simply, *Forever wild*. Ken had arrived in one of the loneliest places that an already solitary human being could go in an increasingly lonely world. He was glad; it beat being in a ghost town.

☐

Wet winds gusted, but he was sheltered. He scratched his face and watched the flames. "Scritchy," Grace used to tease. She'd rub her cheeks hard against his bristles. He was the picture of the backwoods loner: a misanthrope in layers of clothes that all smelled like campfire smoke and dried sweat, his tee shirt faded, the wool jacket stiff with dry mud and the smell of damp lanolin.

The perfect cliché. Shaggy hair, overweight, six feet two inches tall when he bothered to stand erect and wasn't slouching so as not to intimidate other people.

No one to intimidate here. Ken had seen fewer and fewer people as the summer ended. In the last week he'd passed a total of two single hikers, a family, and a couple. Everyone had raised their hands in greeting and headed down the trail to the next pond or on their way back out.

On the day before, he had shared the wet trail for a few minutes with a female park ranger. He imagined how he'd looked: muddy boots, soaked hiking pants, brushing the rain out of his eyes.

He could picture himself, and suddenly Ken did. Across the fire a man stood in the shadows, with rain streaming off a poncho and dripping around his feet.

"Sorry to break into your privacy like this," the stranger said. "You were lost in thought. According to my map this was the nearest lean-to. I'll keep going; it's not dark yet."

"No need to. This is a night for fish, not people," Ken told him.

"Come on. I know you hiked back in here for the solitude."

Ken pointed at the lean-to's back wall. "Stow your gear by mine. Seriously. It's been raining on and off since yesterday. The nighttime is no time to slog on a wet trail. And it won't kill me to spend a night in the company of another person," he added. "I haven't had a real conversation in months. The last person I said hello to was a park ranger. Ken."

"Hey, Ken." The stranger took the proffered hand and shook it. "Malcolm Thatcher. No relation to the Iron Lady." He stepped up into the shelter and ducked under the clothesline Ken had strung at the back of the lean-to. Malcolm shrugged out of his wet poncho.

"Hang it anywhere there's a free nail," Ken suggested.

Malcolm did, and unclipped his small pack and set it against the wall. He patted a yellow pouch hanging around his neck, making sure it was still in place. Malcolm took a seat in front of the fire pit beside Ken and set down a paper bag. Everything he wore was soaked through.

"Nothing dry with you?"

"I didn't bring any extra stuff."

Ken rummaged through a duffel and pulled out a mismatched sweatshirt and sweatpants. "Wear these till your things dry off."

"Thanks. The storm caught me off guard." The sweatshirt and pants fit, and the two eyed one another, bemused. They were both fifteen pounds overweight, with the scruffy beards of men who had sworn off shaving.

"Since you're here, how about some trout rolled in corn meal and fried in grease?"

"Are you kidding? My grandfather used to prepare fish like that. The best taste in the world!" Malcolm smacked his lips. "I just have," he opened the paper bag, "these. I got them at the Pinewood Diner before they closed. They were going to be the last things I ate tonight." He set out two sandwiches and candy bars, chips, and fruit.

"You know," said Ken, "we just might get along."

## II: Day One: Sliding Rock

Malcolm woke to the calling of geese. He could hear them from where he drowsed inside the warm sleeping bag. He kept his eyes closed, listening. A vee must be cutting across the skies heading south, honking as they flew over the Adirondacks from somewhere in Canada.

When he opened his eyes, he was alone in the lean-to. Ken's sleeping bag was rolled up and set at the back wall. The fire was out. Malcolm turned on his other side: his wet clothes from the night before were folded in a neat, dry pile beside his head. He sat up, stretching his arms overhead, and put the clothes back on.

He walked barefoot to a spot ten feet away and stepped into the woods. The air was clean with the singular clarity that comes after a night of heavy rain. "At least I still piss with vigor," he murmured. "No matter what else is wrong with me." He turned back to the lean-to as Ken emerged from a spot in the woods too. "Morning," Malcolm greeted, raising his voice.

"You good?"

"Slept like a log. Thanks again for the fire and a place to lay my head, I mean that."

"No worries. That storm lasted most of the night! Besides," Ken added, "the rule is that campers share the lean-to."

"Rule or not, I'm mighty grateful. I'll get on out of your hair as soon as I have a cup of coffee, if that's all right."

"I used the last coffee days ago and wasn't ready to hike back out for more."

"I've got some. I took it from the last hotel I stayed in." Malcolm fished a couple individual packets of dark roast out of his pack. "It's instant," he qualified.

Ken didn't smile, but his face lit up. "It's coffee!" Ken got the fire going again.

They drank Malcolm's coffee and shared a breakfast of oatmeal and bacon. When they finished, the sun stood at mid-morning in the horizon. The forest was damp; the day was clear and fine.

"I thought I'd hike on into Sliding Rock or High Falls if the day looked good. And it does," said Ken. "You in a hurry?"

"I guess I'm not, not anymore.... I wasn't planning on being on the back trails for long."

"Have you been to Sliding Rock? No?" Ken cracked a slight smile. "It's something to see."

□

Trails in the Adirondack seldom allow hikers to walk abreast. Ken led the way, slowing to accommodate Malcolm's less swift pace. He and Malcolm were the same height, and their rhythms on the trails synchronized in minutes.

They hiked half a mile without talking. "I'm trying to figure out the smell here," Malcolm remarked, finally breaking the silence. "It smells like drying mud, or pine needles gone to loam."

"It's green. The Adirondacks smell is a dark green, or maybe winterberry. My wife always bought balsa incense to burn when we got back home. She swore *that* smelled like the Adirondacks."

They fell silent, each lost in his own thoughts or enjoying the profound and simple activity of walking a trail. Malcolm spoke again awhile later. "A body has to work pretty hard to get this far back in the woods. Cripes, there's barely any infrastructure in some towns this far north."

Up in front of him Ken nodded. "You have to be born in upstate or spend a lot of time here on family vacations. Or," he added seriously, "be a weirdo who likes solitude."

They traversed a hillock over a pond built by a beaver colony. The fall colors were in their full glory in the wilderness, the trees' leaves brilliant scarlet and orange. Recently gnawed and densely interwoven branches dammed the pond. They began walking across the creatures' home.

A beaver lifted his head as they approached. It trundled into the water and swam for the far end. His tail slapped the surface to warn of their presence.

"That beaver probably hasn't seen a human in a while. My God, the leaves! They're something, aren't they? I can't remember a prettier autumn," Ken remarked.

"I've never seen a New England fall. Man, I've never seen trees this color."

"Well," said Ken, not a trace of irony in his voice, "maybe this is one good thing to come out of the coronavirus. We get the trails to ourselves all year now and not just because it's late in the season. I always liked it here because you rarely ran into anyone anyway, even during high season."

"I bet you never shared this spot with a group of obnoxious drunks playing bad music from boom boxes."

"Those days are done and gone."

They crossed the dam and the trail returned as they entered a meadow. Tall grasses came to their waists. The path was still narrow, and Malcolm stayed a constant five feet behind Ken.

"It's funny."

"What?"

"Walking the trail and staying a certain distance in back. You can keep pace with whoever is ahead of you but not get too close. Another thing the coronavirus was good training for."

Ken put out both arms and ran his hands over the tops of the grasses, enjoying the feel of their seed heads against his palms. "Social distancing. For an eternal loner it wasn't so bad. Until suddenly it was."

"How's that?"

Ken changed the topic. "What brings you to the Adirondacks?" Malcolm didn't respond, and Ken was about to turn around and repeat the question.

"I'm in transit," Malcolm finally answered. "I'm supposed to be on my way to Germany. My plane leaves in a couple of weeks. But the real reason I'm here is my parents. My mom was from Canada and when they wanted to get married, it was during the Vietnam War. It made sense for them to move north. I grew up on the prairies. Mom died of a heart attack at age fifty-six. Later, when I asked my father if he missed their earlier life in the US, he gave a name: Cow Horn."

Now Ken did turn around. "Cow Horn Junction?"

"Cow Horn Pond, where they spent their honeymoon. I have no idea how big it is or what it even looks like now."

"Small and beautiful. How funny it's somewhere your parents knew," Ken said quietly.

"Not much to go on as far as names go, is it? Dad died from the virus two years ago. When I got the job in Germany, in the process of packing I came across some falling-apart photo albums he'd passed on to me. One night, I sat with a beer and a joint and started flipping through them. In the back of the oldest album was a shot of a pond in the woods. There was a second photo, the same spot, my parents standing in front of a tent looking incredibly young. I'd never seen the pictures before; I didn't even know they existed. On the back of the first one he'd written, Cow Horn, NY. On the second one the words, the best week of our lives. And out of nowhere came a desire to retrace their steps. I got stubborn in the sort of *so what if I didn't do this when he was still around and could tell me about it* way. I found Cow Horn on a surveyor's map and decided to see it before I headed to Europe. Even the isolation sounded good. I could choose it, without being forced into it."

"There's something about knowing that no matter what time of year you visit, the entire park belongs to you and a couple other souls. Forever wild."

"Nice term," Malcolm agreed.

They came to the end of the meadow and reentered the woods to hike another forty-five minutes in silence. Ken suddenly exclaimed.

"Indian pipe!" He left the trail and made a bee line deeper into the forest.

Malcolm followed and the men squatted on their heels under the trees.

Clumps of strange pale stems rose from the leaf litter of the forest floor. Each stalk was three to five inches high, topped with a single, translucent white petal shaped like a narrow pipe.

Malcolm squinted, trying to understand what he was seeing. "No leaves?"

"Nope. No photosynthesis, and no chlorophyll."

"No photosynthesis? How does that work?"

"The pipes feed on a fungus from the tree roots. That's why they're so ghostly looking," Ken explained. "White, at best pale pink. I've seen specimens of both. We're lucky to see these! Indian pipe grows in the spring and fall, only after it rains. The rainstorm paid off." He stood again and dusted his hands on his jeans.

Maybe because he was pleased to have spotted the elusive flowers, back on the trail Ken opened up a little. He had job hopped: for decades he worked as a bartender, his favorite job. In 2021 he and his wife moved to Alaska. They worked in a seafood cannery for a year. More recently he made fast money in the Dakotas, but in the end hated everything to do with fracking.

As if afraid he'd given away too many details, the flow of personal information stopped and Ken changed the subject.

"So, what's the view of the US these days?"

Malcolm followed behind him and ruminated aloud. "Honestly? Where do I even begin…. Canadians and the rest of the world still have a love-hate relationship with this country. You embody all that's good and bad, in such bloody extremes! What the world thinks depends a lot on who the President is. And, lately? Another failed virus shutdown? Americans get described as incredibly spoiled, dimwitted even. The rest of us figured out how to deal with the virus a couple years ago. Anywhere else on the globe is safer than here.

"No offense, but you asked," he apologized.

Ken waved a hand to indicate it was okay. "Children, we want what we want when we want it."

"Clearly, you guys are overworked and burned out. But we have universal health care and intact social nets. Americans keep suffering, dying like flies, and it's just, wow. Wow. For the first time since Nine Eleven we feel sorry for you. This is somehow different, though. The virus still lurks everywhere, but I tell you true when I say that we think, *Thank God I'm not American.* If this isn't a shift in global perception, nothing is."

Ken's body tensed, but reluctantly he nodded. "It's the Great American Nightmare. No more refusing to wake up from it, though. Not anymore."

"So, let me ask, any thoughts on how the changes will shake out?"

"I've been in the woods for months. I have no idea what's happening out there. What can I say? Change was long overdue." He fell silent; there was nothing to add.

They kept hiking, and abruptly the trail ended at the bottom of a flat, slick piece of stone.

Malcolm stared, gawping in astonishment. "What the hell?"

Trees grew along the banks of a loud stream and the sides

of the long stone. A torrent rushed down a sloped rockslide. Dark water pooled at the bottom.

Ken answered obliquely as he led Malcolm up a path trod in the grass alongside the slanting stone. "If the next shortages are going to be clean air and water, this spot's well stocked. The area got record snowfall last winter."

They followed the path to the top.

"It's at least twenty feet wide!" Malcolm exclaimed.

"It is. Welcome to Sliding Rock Falls. They used to say, 'do not venture past this point in these woods without a guide'. Meet you at the bottom," Ken announced, pretending he didn't see the alarmed look on Malcolm's face as he stripped to his boxer shorts. Ken stepped out onto the rock, sat, and pushed off with a deep bellow as the rushing waters caught his body and tugged him along. He slid down the rock and landed with a splash in the pool, still yelling.

"It's cold!" he shouted to where Malcolm was getting ready to follow his example. "There's a bump at the bottom! In the middle, a little to the right of the middle of the rock, go around or go airborne!"

Malcolm almost slipped as he stepped onto the wet rockslide. He regained his balance, took a few more steps, almost fell again. He sat on his ass and scooted his way out to the middle.

When he screamed as he slid, Malcolm sounded like a seven-year-old boy.

The two of them climbed out of the pool and back up the path tamped in the grass. They slid over and over, whooping like kids. When they finally stopped, out of breath and chilled, Ken had bruises from where he had found that bump in the slide (not where he'd remembered it as being after all).

"This place is unreal!" laughed Malcolm. His lips were blue.

"Oh, it's real alright." Ken grinned.

It was the first time Malcolm had seen him really smile.

*Ken's a serious guy,* he thought, *I hadn't noticed he never laughs. Oh, he's cordial, God knows it's super that he let me crash at his camp site. Yeah, cordial enough, and probably glad to have someone to talk with again. But, is he a guy who smiles easily? No way.*

The men sat on their tee shirts as they dried off. They rested near the top of the slide. The afternoon filled with the sound of running waters and the calls of occasional birds.

Ken leaned back on his elbows and tried not to stare. With their wet hair slicked back out of their faces, he and Malcolm had strikingly similar profiles. Both were bearded men with stocky builds. As they sat a few feet away from one another, they might have been brothers.

But there the similarities ended. The base of Malcolm's throat was a mass of recent scar tissue.

Malcolm caught Ken staring and reflexively raised a hand to hide his neck. "Tracheotomy," he said quietly. "Complications. They had to intubate me. I caught the virus and landed in a Toronto plague ward. There I was." He shook himself hard all over like a dog trying to get dry. "In an isolation unit, and all my plans suddenly didn't matter. Everything in my life had been in motion. I was going places… until I wasn't. I spent all my waking hours thinking about the way I was going to die."

He went silent, gazing at the icy water rushing over the rock. "Is the water always this cold?"

"Actually, it's still got some summer heat in it. But, here, yeah, getting in the water is a cold plunge."

Malcolm was shivering as he wrapped his sweatshirt around his shoulders. "They had me hooked up to a ventilator in the intensive care unit. That's where I spent my birthday last winter."

"How old?"

"Forty-five."

"Me too: August 19th. I spent my birthday here." Ken grasped gratefully at each chance to shift the conversation;

the virus had brought so much illness and death into the world. The men could restore balance and a sense of normality with conversations about water temperature, about birthdays.

He heaved himself to his feet. "Well," he began to dress again, "we should probably start back."

## III: Day One: Malcolm's Tale

On the return trail another looping conversation began.

"So, what's your 2020?" Malcolm asked. He didn't need to elaborate. The phrase "What's your 2020?" had entered the universal lexicon. A disparate, divided world had experienced the initial crisis as one, and together shared the hardships and loneliness brought on by lockdowns. "What's your 2020?" was understood to inquire, *How was your life upended? Did you survive intact?*

"Mine didn't have a happy ending," Ken said in a low voice. "Tell me yours."

Malcolm briskly said, "It's a funny question. It became international overnight, didn't it?"

"That it did."

Malcolm thought for a minute before he spoke and used his hands to talk even though Ken couldn't see them. "I'm on my way to a job with a German outfit, working the wind energy rigs in the North Sea. I was accepted for a factory job in the south, too, building hybrid cars. Double luck! Even in 2025 Germany is always one of those national economies that keeps purring along. My work visa's as a Canadian. Can you imagine the mess *that* would be as a Brit?"

"Being from Canada is good," Ken agreed. "My family was Canadian for a little while – a couple centuries ago. Skedaddlers, people called them. They headed over the border because they had stayed loyal to King George and didn't want any part of the War of Independence. More likely, they were fur traders who knew the trapping lines were about to run out. They hedged their bets; I wish I had."

The two hiked in the comfortable silence of men who like one another.

"I took the job," Malcolm resumed, "I accepted the position, consolidated my belongings and shipped everything. I kept thinking about my parents, so I decided to come here before I go. Since the virus took my dad, nothing's left holding me in Canada anyway. I planned this whole transition around a trip here in the wilderness. You can't imagine the forestry practices of countries like Germany. The Black Forest is lovely, but man is it managed."

Ken threw a look over his shoulder. "When you like wilderness, any wild place is good. But your first love is the one you spend your childhood in. My wife Grace was from northern California, and her love went to the giant redwoods. A friend in Arizona swore by high desert, blooming in the spring when it rains."

"Well, this forest is the last hike."

Ken turned around again with his eyebrows raised. "You sound glum." He spoke lightly but couldn't read Malcolm's face.

"Anyway," Malcolm said. "I should get my finished packet in the mail. I *thought* the last task was the passport photos, but I got a letter with a request for new documents. Employers want the coronavirus health status update cards."

"I got one just before I headed into the woods. I keep copies in my vehicle, in my pack, and on a file in the cloud."

The woods suddenly rang with eerie calls.

"A family of loons on a pond, within earshot," Ken said eagerly. "They're talking to one another." The two men fell silent, listening. The birds called in carrying, wailing houoo ouoo oos to one another. Normal language hung, suspended, as the birds' otherworldly voices echoed in the forest.

Ken spoke again only when the conversation of the loons

had completely faded. "Family?" he asked, still thinking of the birds.

"Divorced, no sibs, no kids."

"No emotional baggage then. You're lucky. I'm such a guy. My wife used to yell the words at me. 'You're such a guy!' Because I don't talk about emotions. Fuck that: I'm never going to talk with a therapist. Or go in for couples' counselling. If I didn't want to talk about personal issues with her, or some therapist who's a total stranger, what made Grace think I'd be willing to do it in a group? Supposedly that works for some people. More power to them. I do not belong to that group of people…. I like self isolation, the less I'm forced to give prize to 'what makes me tick' the better. You know what I mean?"

"I sure do! Women need words, explanations," said Malcolm. "My mom was unbelievable. She started conversations all the time with perfect strangers, bus stops, at the mall, waiting in line for a table, she'd tell them painfully intimate details about her health issues and stuff. Although I have to say, she made friends really easy."

This was perfect trail talk.

"Exactly." Ken happily expanded on his theory. "Not men. I like you or I don't like you, you're an idiot and I knew this about you the minute you entered the room. We shook hands, you opened your mouth, and you confirmed what I already knew."

"It's like looking at women. When a woman is sexy, you know," Malcolm stated. "Maybe it's the way she smells, and not necessarily whether or not she's wearing perfume. It might be the way she smiles. Private. Like, she knows a secret and the rest of the world isn't quick enough or smart enough to catch on yet. It can be the way she moves. I'll watch her walking away and bro, trust me. I am *not* having coherent thoughts. My reptilian brain stem is doing the responding. And, how guys relate? An old friend once admitted: 'I thought you were a world-class asshole when I first met you'. He told me this with a slap on the shoulder, 'don't take it the wrong way, I'm telling you this because now I don't think it.'"

"Yeah," said Ken. "When you showed up drowning last night, I made a snap decision. I figured I'd probably be able to stand your company for a night or two."

### IV: Day Two: Cow Horn Pond

Malcolm took the trail in to visit Cow Horn Pond the next day by himself.

That night both were quiet. Ken looked up from the notebook he was writing in when Malcolm returned. A can of stew was warming on the fire.

"Cow Horn what you'd hoped?"

Malcolm sat beside him and pulled off the yellow pouch he always wore around his neck. He unzipped it and wordlessly removed two curling photographs.

Ken examined the old pictures. Cow Horn Pond. A pair of hippies in front of a small tent on the edge of the water. Carefully he turned them over to read the inscriptions on the backs and then returned the photos to Malcolm.

"It was like a time machine. The colors, the look of the pond, it looked like nothing has changed."

"It hasn't," Ken said gently, "it never does. That's why I love it."

□

By unspoken agreement, Malcolm put off leaving. What part did the coronavirus play in the spontaneous decision to hang out together? After consecutive waves of the virus, life felt different. Everyone was in this together, willing or not. The only certainty was that within ninety seconds of meeting one another in a lean-to on a back trail, both Ken and Malcolm recognized a brother in arms.

It is startling to realize even a self-imposed and carefully cultivated isolation occasionally needs to be broken. On a trail, conversations bounce from quiet contemplation to debates about the meaning of life - or the world's best beer. A chance meeting with a human being with whom you can share isolation – and remain in that bubble even as you allow another person to experience the quiet with you – is rare. They appear as rarely as Indian pipe or hearing the ghostly call of loons. If you are gifted with such an encounter, you welcome it.

For Ken there was, as well, the knowledge that soon Malcolm would be back on the trail. Their chance encounter was short and posed no obligations.

Indian summer was on its last glorious, dying legs, the weather shifting to cool and rainy late autumn. It was almost time for Ken to leave the woods and take the trail out returning to civilization, whatever that looked like now.

No job, no one waiting for him, the future a gigantic unknown.

He had to reacclimate to society. Before he returned to the world, he should approach cautiously, take his time. He needed to think like a deep-sea diver, rising gradually back to the surface and not get the bends. A few days with another human being while still in the forest was a safe way to do that.

### V: Day Three: The Trail to High Falls

They started early for High Falls the next morning. It was a lengthier trek and they enjoyed the hike, taking their time. Ken slowly grew more talkative. He picked up an earlier, personal conversation thread; it was easier with the woods in front of him and his listener behind him. "The best job I ever had was tending bar at a place called JJ's. I worked with a guy by the name of Gabe Burgess. Gabe was the best-traveled person I ever met, or ever will…. He liked to travel, and he loved the chance to experience the new and unknown. Gabe was always taking a trip to yet another, new, exotic corner of the world. He was real easy going. Gabe was a *great* bartender, he genuinely liked people and he was a big enough guy that people in the bar never got stupid.

"When everyone could go back out for meals and to meet friends again, our bar was full. From the minute our doors opened. And the weird thing is, it wasn't like people wanted to get blind drunk, it was the need to be in a place with other people where all of you were a bit lit, and you looked at one another with wonder. Even those who *weren't* fine-looking got hugged. All that nonsense about looks had been swept away. Too many people had loved ones who were going to be attached to tubes for months, or maybe forever.

"Yeah, people drank because they were overcome. They stood or sat at JJ's and drank, toasted the folks sitting at the nearest table and meant it, really meant it. The question you asked the other day, what's your 2020? That was when mine started, at JJ's when the first wave seemed like it had ended. We cared about each other's stories. I saw friends I hadn't called or written, but I'd maybe thought about them in the middle of a day in the middle of the lockdown, hey, I wonder how Chris is doing, I should call him or send an email. And suddenly it was evening and another day in quarantine had passed by and damn it, another day where I hadn't done anything except float in a strange in-between parallel universe. So, if I saw somebody I'd thought of but hadn't contacted, all I could do was give them a hug and say, You were on my mind during the lockdown! How are you doing? Everyone safe?

"There's not even a flicker in the other person's eyes, because let's cut through the bull: we're trying to survive a mass extermination. As long as we weren't on the endangered species list, who cared? But we are on the list, along with everything else on the planet.

"Shit, where was I? Bartending. Gabe and JJ's are extended family. It's teamwork. Once you've worked there, a job is always yours if you want it. So, I wasn't too worried about what was going to happen. Grace and I headed to Alaska in 2021 to look for somewhere quiet and work in the fisheries. Turned out the environmental safeguards had been removed, and there was a tanker disaster...."

Rat a tat tat to their left. Rat a tat tat from the right. Off in the woods, a pair of woodpeckers bored for insects in tree boles on both sides of the trail.

"We returned in 2022 to the lower forty-eight and the virus returned, another mutation. I called my old bosses, who said JJ's was back to doing home deliveries and takeaway. Then I talked to Gabe, and I could barely hear his voice. He said this was going to be worse, far worse. He told us to head back to somewhere quiet, stay safe and healthy, and take care of one another.

"He was crying. The coolest human being I ever met hung up on me. Yeah, that kind of colored my own response to what was happening. If only we'd followed Gabe's advice."

Ken didn't say another word until they reached High Falls two hours later. "I'm not ready for this story after all. Maybe tonight."

### VI: Day Three: Ken's 2020

Back at the lean-to, they ate a supper of canned corned beef hash and roasted potatoes. "Don't even think about compensating me for the food," Ken warned. "This is basic hospitality." Ken could not explain or articulate it, but he knew Malcolm was the unexpected sacred guest of every culture's folklore.

Ken waited until it was completely dark. He gazed into his tin coffee cup as the flames of the fire sparked. "You still want it, I'll tell you the rest of my story." He waited until Malcolm nodded, and plunged back into his tale.

"My losses started late in 2022. Yeah, my mom was over eighty anyway, but that didn't mean it was a good thing when her senior housing became a hot spot of the renewed epidemic. I couldn't even say goodbye.

"Cities in some regions had begun the work of repairing broken social contracts. We had moved to California, found work and hunkered down. Grace and I were debt-o-phobic, and we'd banked everything we earned in Alaska. At the start of 2023 another mutation hit, and both of us were furloughed. We burned through our savings with health care costs and a day came when we had trouble paying the rent. The electricity bill. The heat bill. Our water bill. Hell, even the garbage bill. No more bail out money, because the economy was back up and running, right?

"I got hired back on, let go again.

"We lost my brother-in-law, Tremaine. He caught the new coronavirus strain and he died. A couple of months later Tremaine's wife Kerry Ann died. Cory and Elias, my nephews, survived. That particular wave of the virus turned the boys into orphans." Ken turned his face away; for a few minutes dry wood hissed and sparked as he added branches to the fire.

Malcolm didn't speak, knowing that there was more. Much more.

"What's the proper response when children are orphaned but there's no agency left with space to care for them? What's the right thing to do? Grace and I took the kids in. I was rehired - finally. Life almost returned to normal… and half a year later Grace died. We'd gotten infected in the second wave of the pandemic and thought we were immune. Not to the mutated virus. When she got sick, this time it killed her.

"I re-lost the job, a third time, that time for good. It wasn't coming back. I talked the situation over with both boys; we were making any decisions as family of equals. God knows they became as grownup as those of us who were trying to protect them. When a cousin on their dad's side offered to adopt the kids, we all voted yes. It seemed like the only choice. I sold everything of value and set up a trust fund for them with most of it. I put the last of my personal belongings in a storage unit and began driving east early in 2024, looking for work. And here I am a year later, with my brand new, virus infection-free status papers and identity card, and not one single prospect for a job with health benefits or job security. By the way, if you want to communicate via Internet, this area still has no reception. In case you weren't aware."

"I was," said Malcolm. He was relieved by the conversation shift; Ken's truths were hard to listen to even so far back in the woods. "It's why I'm here. Not a lot I want to be in contact with anymore, you know?"

"Yeah. I hike out if I need supplies. I do a lot of fishing and yes, I bought a license. Some aspects of being a member of civilization need to be honored. I know I can't stay in this campsite forever, but it feels as if I've always lived in the back woods and this is all I'll ever need. Summertime was easy. Talking with other folks would just make me miss the ones who are gone. It's taken months of being by myself; I can accept that they aren't coming back.

"There isn't going to be a bright side to this crisis. We're in a loop, and it'll keep repeating over and over. And over, until people finally see that we're driving ourselves out of existence."

"Parts of the country are changing. Parts are healing. And people need hope, because without hope they kill themselves," Malcolm interrupted.

"I'm not done with my story," Ken kept on talking, relentless. "Nowhere near done. I was one of those people who had hope. I kept driving and went back to work, a warehouse job in the Midwest last year. Yeah, people are reorganizing unions and hiring without looking at race, religion or sex. I was relieved to be working again.

"But people I met kept getting sick, and I was scared shitless I was next. A woman I knew back in my old life, the co-owner and chef at JJ's, used to shrug her shoulders and roll her eyes when we talked about changing the world. Never underestimate the power of denial, she'd say in this cryptic voice. But I still had hope." A pause, followed by the rasp of Ken clearing his throat in order to go on speaking. "You mentioned Nine Eleven the other day. That event brought on a pain that *really* hurt, it was a massive aching for the innocent people in those twin towers and trapped on the planes. And genuine horror that somebody had planned that, the malignant patience, I mean, it's beyond imagining.

"COVID-19 happened all over the world. No one *planned* it. When Grace died and I had to leave the boys, that world rushed back in. I had waves of pain I couldn't believe, they came and went, they were super random. I'd be sober and wham! Here was this pain. Or I'd be in the middle of my second beer, not even buzzed and wham! There it was again. I went through a phase where it was a struggle to even function, so I stayed wasted. For months I lived in a deep, dark void. No way I could deal with the unrest and despair everywhere. And the losses that ended life as I once knew it, forever." Ken stopped talking. "Give me a minute," he choked.

Malcolm got up, went to his pack, and fished around inside it for a bottle. He filled their coffee cups with the tequila.

Ken drained his cup in one swallow and held it out for a refill.

Malcolm poured more. He waited.

"Yeah…the world rushed back in. I couldn't talk about how I felt. Feel. And I had no idea how to deal with that. I watched the usual evening news about the millions of people who died. Most countries had beaten the virus, and now these were reports on the impact it had left.

"One night I saw a special report, personal interviews with grieving parents and friends and spouses, and the clip was an illiterate peasant, talking about the way he felt after losing his entire extended family. He spoke words a thousand times more eloquent than anything I could imagine saying; he said what I couldn't. I began hunting for those reports, how people had reacted when they got slammed with the virus. There's always a person who breaks down during the interview and starts sobbing. That's the one I waited for. I can't cry, but I experience catharsis watching somebody on the television or my laptop screen lose it. Watching *them* fall apart emotionally means I don't need to. I can put it off for another day.

"I couldn't watch enough of these reports. It's not like I thought, it'll never be me crying. I know I can't project my issues onto them and say they're the people who can't accept the reality of what the coronavirus took away. Or that if I experience it second hand by watching them fall apart, I won't have to. No… when I watched them and heard their stories, I felt their pain. Not my pain. Theirs. It was the weirdest displaced identity. *I was those other people.*

"It didn't make a shred of difference what color they were, or their religion, or their age, or even their sex. Old, young and in-between, for those few minutes or hours, I was that color, that religion, that sex and that age, I fit myself inside their skins like I'd inhabited them all along. It wasn't identification with, it was me completely sharing in that person's experiences.

"It wasn't appropriation," Ken added. "It was: merging.

The one thing I can't do is cry. If I did, I'm afraid I'd never stop.

"Now I'm in the wilderness, no contact with the outside world for months until you showed up. It's just been me and my losses, and my pain. I was left with myself... I had to become myself again. And that's okay. I think a lot about those reports I watched, and the suffering around the world. I get it, you know? At forty-five years old, I get it finally, we are all connected, we're just one big organism. The boundaries of skin and country and otherness are constructs used to confuse us."

"I don't know, Ken. I definitely feel alone."

"Look, I have plenty of skills and life experience and no one left to share them with. My life was nothing really but the routine of getting up, going to work, coming home to Grace or the boys. I miss that life. I had the perfect woman. I wonder if I'm just passing the time now until I get to be with her again. If there is an afterlife. I hope there is." Ken shook his head, thinking about something he didn't mention.

Malcolm didn't ask him to elaborate; he refilled their cups with tequila but remained silent.

"The country goes in and out of lockdown, and when I'm not in lockdown I volunteer at shelters and help register people to vote. It's ironic as hell, because I don't have a permanent address myself anymore! That's what I mean when I say I finally get it. We are all connected, in unfathomable ways, in a sense beyond anything I even pretend I understand. Everything parsed to the ultimate meaning. The barest of minimums." Ken leaned forward to put another branch on the fire. "I have the right antibodies for every mutation. And boy, are my blood cells in high demand. Clinics pay top dollar, so I give blood as often as I'm allowed to.

"One last story, and I'll be done. On my drive cross country, early this spring I worked on a building crew for a few weeks. There was a cave-in. A sinkhole took out a block.

"Ever seen a sinkhole up close? One night you lay in your bed asleep and the next thing you know, the walls collapse and you and your bed are sucked into this gaping hole that was forming there all along. Once a sinkhole goes, there's no stopping it.

"Those homeowners should have gotten a chance to rebuild, but the building permits were a mess. The government gutted all the provisions and oversights that used to keep speculators from exploiting whatever they want.

"I'm losing the thread, sorry…. Slices of the world fall off and the bastards walk away the minute there's nothing left to be extracted. They just step back a little further from the edge they brought into being. And meanwhile the earth under our feet is shifting and falling away in slices. In chunks.

"The site caught on fire, too. When the fires finished burning all that remained were bitter ashes, like the kind used to mark people's foreheads at Lent. For whatever that analogy might be worth.

"That job finished, and I kept heading East. I drove here on autopilot. The Adirondacks! Some towns are a little more prosperous, most a whole lot less. The usual closed local shops and failed businesses. Same story everywhere. But this," – his arms swept out wide to include the fire-lit interior of the lean-to, and the dark woods beyond – "is for eternity." Ken's eyes softened and he pressed his lips together in a smile that was beautiful, and sad. "Sorry for the way I've rambled, it's been so long since I had someone to talk to. But my 2020 never really ended, and try as I will, I have no idea what I will do next. But it's time I get on the trail back out."

## VII: Day Four: The Trail Back Out

Malcolm helped Ken replenish the store of brushwood piled just inside the entry to the lean-to. "Backwoods etiquette. It's not just for me when I get back later," Ken explained as he made a stack of kindling. "You never know when you'll get caught in the elements or reach shelter after it's gotten dark. If someone else comes along and needs a fire, everything's ready for them."

"I'll miss this," Malcolm said, and he stood for a minute before they left the clearing.

They decided to take a break when they reached the trailhead. Ken opened the wooden box and pulled out the register to sign himself out. "You didn't sign in?" He looked for Malcolm's name on the sheet but couldn't find it.

"I walked right past the trailhead sign on purpose. Didn't want to be identified. Stupid, I know. Stupid."

"Well, you can do it now."

"A last autograph for the world," Malcolm muttered.

"How's that?"

Malcolm signed the curling page of the lined notebook and set it with the pencil back into the wooden box. He closed the lid.

The men sat side by side on a nurse log, sharing a meal of leftover breakfast trout and apples that Ken cut into slices with his pocketknife. "On the back trails, the last thing you want is to listen to someone blathering on. It was good having you to talk with the last three days," he said unexpectedly.

Malcolm laughed. "It's not like you exactly talked my head off at first. When I first saw you sitting in the lean-to, I felt bad about invading your privacy. I was surprised when you offered me the chance to crash there."

"It was raining, Malcolm." Ken's tone was dry. "You didn't look like a serial killer and it was seriously pouring. But, yeah…. I don't ask as many questions as I did pre-virus. I make better snap decisions. Now I write Elias and Cory, telling them what I do each day. Every so often I make myself hike out to mail what I've written. And call them.

Eight and ten years old, a million years wise and doing well despite everything. They're my hopes for the future. Hey, you need a lift somewhere? I parked my car by the bridge. I can drive you; I need to head to Blue Lake." Ken surprised himself with the offer, but no matter which town he chose to go shopping in, he had to sacrifice a day to getting more provisions.

Slowly Malcolm took his time swallowing; slowly he spoke. "Here's the thing. Once we part ways, I'm hiking back in. I'm taking the trail back in as far as I can go before it gets dark." His voice contracted. "I was all ready to send off my papers to Germany. The last item was a fresh passport, issued on the spot now at the airport. I filled out the forms and was ready to go. But no, the last item turns out to be a health certificate, stamped that I'm virus-free. My employer needs proof of a medical exam done in the last two months.

"That scar you saw, the tracheotomy? I went through double pneumonia, pleurisy, you name it. I look okay, but it left my heart and lungs permanently damaged. I might need an operation at some point.

"I considered lying. Just submit my old documents and head off to Europe anyway. But that won't work either, because international regulations require that a doctor does another complete workup on-site. Safety regulations."

All around them spread the yielding, pine-scented floor of the Adirondack woods.

"I kept putting off getting a physical. I was too busy with the shipping arrangements." In a soft voice he added, "I'll never get that international health certificate now."

He and Ken stared wordless at one another as they sat on the decaying log. Eventually Malcolm went on.

"Everyone who travels has to carry the International Identification COVID-19 Health Status papers. If I apply, I'll get a stamp that warns I have permanent health issues. Or, worse: that I need to stay in place.

"My doctor back in Canada assures me that if I take it easy and stay on meds for the rest of my life, I'll probably live out the expected lifespan for a male virus survivor of my age and health markers. The expected lifespan! Whatever that means post-2020." Malcolm's face was a cipher. "The answer for me changed in a heartbeat. *Certainly* not a pun. I can't take the job." Suddenly, he screamed at the top of his compromised lungs. "Fuck! This was not what I had in mind!" He stopped, out of breath. "I hadn't planned on these last couple days. It's like meeting you gave me the chance to say goodbye. I'm hiking back in," he resumed in a clearer voice, his tone now new, serene. Malcolm pulled the pouch out from his shirt, unzipped it, and removed the photographs of his parents at Cow Horn Pond. "I'm going to commit suicide. That night we met? I was going to do it the next morning." Malcolm closed the pouch and set it on the log between the two of them. "I had it all planned. First, I was going to eat a last meal and drink the bottle of tequila. I would spend a last night in a sleeping bag under the stars at Cow Horn Pond, but the storm stopped me. Today, I'll get as far back in the woods as I can go before it's dark, and when I get there, I'll do it."

"Damn. You plan to kill...." The sentence died away unfinished. "Do you know how much time you've got left?"

"The doctors couldn't say."

"Couldn't, or wouldn't?"

"Ethically they aren't allowed to give you your death sentence. But I think they really can't tell me, this virus's mutations jangled life expectations and morbidity predictions. I was invited to partake in the huge international study. They would monitor my medications and evaluate changes in my health outcomes. Something like that. I couldn't see it, sitting around in an empty city and wondering when - if - it was going to come back, and wondering if I was going to. Everything I own is sailing to Hamburg. All the paperwork's right here." He patted the pouch.

"Is the State Department still closed?"

"No, it reopened last month. The World Health Organization is helping governments validate international passports. The process only takes a week, tops." Malcolm picked up the pouch and held it out. "Ken, take this. You say you have nowhere to go. It will be years before this country gets back on its feet. Go on, take my papers. Take my job. All you need is the health exam. The appointment's already set up; just go as me. You can get new passport photos made. I've made my peace." He set the pouch back on the nurse log and gazed off into the forest. "You still have options."

☐

Ken touched the pouch but couldn't bring himself to pick it up. "You really plan to kill...." He stared out into the same trees, tried twice more to speak, had to stop himself each time. At last, he got out his notebook, and carefully he tore out the last three pages. "I'm writing down my boys' address and a general to whom it may concern note if anyone questions you."

Now Malcolm remained silent, not moving, not even seeming to breathe as Ken concentrated on composing the notes.

"This is the address for my storage locker." A key dangled from the end of a chain Ken pulled from a closed jacket pocket. "Take whatever you think you can use. And these." Ken dug into another jacket pocket for his wallet and removed all the plastic cards. "Take them. Please," he requested. "If I become you... you can become me." He wrote out another half page. "The passwords for my bank accounts and credit cards. And how I sign my signature. Practice that. Better yet, report the cards as stolen and order new ones you can sign yourself. The money in the accounts can keep you going for the time you have left."

He piled everything in Malcolm's hands and held his gaze. "Take these and be me. It's your decision and I sure can't tell you what to do. Don't decide this minute; but if you want it, choose to live. We can both go back."

☐

Half an hour later the ranger reached the trailhead. She replaced her water bottle in the side net of her day pack. She was heading back to Cat Mountain Fire Tower. She had met her girlfriend for a weekend at a hotel with a hot shower, queen size bed, and a bar. The ranger hadn't cared about television or the Internet, but the renewed personal contact had been nice.

A man approached her on the trail. He held onto a small, canary yellow pouch as if it were a lifeline, tethering him to the trail back out. She recognized the bearded, overweight guy camping out in the remote lean-to by the back ponds. They had exchanged quiet hellos twice near the fire tower where she was the summer ranger, and she had spotted him with her binoculars from high in the tower as she scanned for fires. She had run into him on the trail a few days ago.

The ranger raised her hand in greeting but quickly dropped it. A solitary human being herself, she knew better than to interrupt another person's private grief. He came closer and she prepared to pass him with a quiet glance of acknowledgment.

Ken lifted his damp face. The tears ran down it unchecked. When he saw her, he began quietly laughing as though he would never stop.

"Hey there," he said. "Hello, world."

## THE BEGINNING

# Afterword

I read many of the stories in this collection at public readings with the Writers in Stuttgart. The readings' themes yielded the following: Better Weather from *Risk*, The River from *Winter Tales*, The Green Under the Snow from *The Kindness of Strangers*, and The Red Wallet from *Secrets from the Writers' Den*. I penned Do Dreams Float? to the theme *Truth or Fiction*. Stuttgart's Dreigroschentheater, Theater am Olgaeck, and Merlin have all hosted us.

Other stories took me longer to write. The first version of Rules to Live By is from 2002. I was experiencing a writing logjam and took a break. I put on my jacket and went for a walk. The scene with the classroom came to me as I headed through the orchards close to our apartment. I returned home and wrote a gorgeous, rewarding chunk of complete imagery.

I wrote Quack Quack a decade ago, right after I met with a friend and her daughter in Venice. A rude tourist really did quack at an old Italian retiree, and a voluble child transformed eerily – and completely – when she donned a traditional Venetian mask.

I waited years to figure out my title story The Trail Back Out. I always had the how, what, and where, but not the why. Then the coronavirus happened, and all the rest of it…. Writing and writer came together in a way I cannot explain. Two strangers met on a remote back trail in real time. I vanished from all the pain and confusion of the world crisis by merging with my story's place and people.

I spent a winter month in Hong Kong and the New Territories, and Mumbai, India. I used that time away from home as a chance to prep my next book project.

Plans coalesced during a holiday Uwe and I took a few weeks later. Daydreaming about this book was a wonderful way to while away the hours as vans carried us around Costa Rica. That trip was perfect, and bliss is a magical place for beginnings.

I stared out windows at the countryside and let my mind wander. Every twenty or thirty minutes, I found myself hauling out a pen and notepaper, taken by an insight. Or random idea. Or connecting detail.

We returned home in March 2020. We were now in 'the year of the corona', that new sign in astrology represented by a microbe with destructive, plutonic energy. Planes stopped flying and less than a week later Germany went into lockdown. I hadn't been home for longer than a few weeks since December 2019. Now I *was* home and had to stay inside. When you are a writer, being forced into a lockdown is one great situation.

The isolation brought by the novel coronavirus was an intense place in which to create. World events rushed in to inform my writing. The stories compressed as I worked on them, and I was morphing and changing as well. These days I feel a hundred years older.

How will we get from Point A to Point B as a planet, as 21st century humans, as Homo Sapiens? We named ourselves *Wise Man*. Will those who follow us still call us that?

The characters in my stories are looking for the trail back out. May we all find our ways. In the end, all trails join.

# ACKNOWLEDGEMENTS

The following people commented on story drafts: Erica Applezweig, Freni Avari, Kavi Avari, Michael Bayba, Nancy Carroll, Lindsey Cole, Victoria Hahn, Michael Hilton, Diana Lopez, Kay Lutz, Pia Newman, Joan Robertson, and Liz Slater. Special thanks to Jim Palik for suggesting I close this book with the words The Beginning.

I belong to two writing groups. The Writers in Stuttgart meet once a month and Wordsmiths & Penmonkeys meet virtually once a week.

Artist Walter Share of waltercolors.com continues to paint my covers. Walter sent me the cover image of Lake Como several years ago. "Write me a story about this painting," he said. Do Dreams Float? is my answer to his challenge.

Uwe Hartmann supplies technical expertise, smart critiques, and emotional backup. He is the haven in all my storms.

I ran every story past my sisters. We chat twice a week, and I always look forward to laughing, exchanging details about our daily lives, or just shooting the breeze. Our calls are timed so that Germany, Oregon, and Oaxaca are all awake and available to talk. Barb and Pam have always been artists. I'm glad I finally made the leap.

## ABOUT THE AUTHOR

Jadi Campbell has lived in Europe since 1992. She writes frequently for NEAT, Stuttgart's New English American Theater.

Her books are *Broken In: A Novel in Stories*, *Tsunami Cowboys*, *Grounded*, and *The Trail Back Out*.

*Broken In: A Novel in Stories* was Semifinalist for the 2020 Hawk Mountain Short Story Collection Award and Finalist for Greece's 2021 Eyelands Book of the Year Award (Short Stories). *Tsunami Cowboys* was longlisted for the 2019 ScreenCraft Cinematic Book Award. *The Trail Back Out* was American Book Fest 2020 Best Book Award Finalist: Fiction Anthologies, 2021 Top Shelf Award Runner-Up, 2021 IAN Book of the Year Award Short Story Collection Finalist and awarded a 2021 Wishing Shelf Red Ribbon. The title story 'The Trail Back Out' was longlisted for the 2021 ScreenCraft Cinematic Short Story Award.

She blogs at www.jadicampbell.com.

Printed in Great Britain
by Amazon